TEMPTING A LONELY LORD

The Rakes of Mayhem
Book 6

Anna St. Claire

DRAGONBLADE PUBLISHING, INC.

ARE YOU SIGNED UP FOR DRAGONBLADE'S BLOG?

You'll get the latest news and information on exclusive giveaways, exclusive excerpts, coming releases, sales, free books, cover reveals and more.

Check out our complete list of authors, too!

No spam, no junk. That's a promise!

Sign Up Here

www.dragonbladepublishing.com

Dearest Reader;

Thank you for your support of a small press. At Dragonblade Publishing, we strive to bring you the highest quality Historical Romance from some of the best authors in the business. Without your support, there is no 'us', so we sincerely hope you adore these stories and find some new favorite authors along the way.

Happy Reading!

CEO, Dragonblade Publishing

Additional Dragonblade books by Author Anna St. Claire

The Rakes of Mayhem Series
The Earl of Excess (Book 1)
The Marquess of Mischief (Book 2)
The Duke of Disorder (Book 3)
The Baron's Return (Book 4)
To Win a Viscount's Heart (Book 5)
Tempting a Lonely Lord (Book 6)
A Gift for Agatha (Novella)

The Lyon's Den Series
Lyon's Prey
The Heart of a Lyon
Once Upon a Winter's Tale (Novella)
A Lyon of Her Own

Also from Anna St. Claire
Once upon a Haunted Heart (Novella)

PROLOGUE

Off the coast of Tintagel, England
Late November 1818

"BLACKSTONE, GIVE UP, now. Your men have either perished, or they've been captured," William said, thrusting his sword at the bald man in a skull cap in front of him.

"Never! This is only an imposition. There are more children where these came from," the man taunted him. "So many children that I can fill ship after ship…"

"Not if I have anything to say about it," William declared as he parried. "You've kidnapped your last child." Blackstone's mud-colored eyes stared back at him. "Admit it! Are you not the Pied Piper?"

"Wouldn't you like to know?" Blackstone said in a gravelly voice.

"We'll find out soon enough. You're under arrest for the attempted smuggling of these children." Any man who stole children and sold them into slavery deserved no compassion. William thrust his sword at the enemy.

Blackstone blocked the strike, the two steel sabers clanging loudly against one another. William stepped back and thrust again.

Blackstone parried and thrust yet again, forcing William to dodge a swipe across his midsection. He noticed the man looking behind him before swinging his blade once more.

The storm raged, violently tossing the small smuggling vessel against the cresting waves, with massive sheets of water washing over the deck. William kept his feet planted on the deck, bracing himself whenever the ship climbed the waves. Rain pelted down as thunder and lightning crashed. Mentally, he tallied the children he had seen brought aboard. According to his count, his men should have transferred all the children to his vessel by now.

William and his men had been watching the man the man they *thought* was the Pied Piper for almost a week, observing his movements and the number of girls and boys he'd kidnapped. But was he the Pied Piper? According to sources, Blackstone was planning to sell the children into slavery in the Ottoman Empire. Thirteen children had been stolen.

There was a special place in hell for people like Blackstone. William would see that the man found his way there.

A sudden wave swept over the ship's side, washing a screaming Blackstone into the rough seas.

The skies grew dark, with lightning flashing to the left and right of the boat. William scanned the waves with his spyglass and spotted the smuggler bobbing in the water, frantically waving for help. Pulling off his jacket, William was readying to jump into the choppy waves to rescue the bastard when a child's voice cried out from the depths of the deck. Stepping away from the railing of the boat, William spun around, listening for the faint voice again. It was windy and rainy, but there was no way he would leave one child behind.

"M-mama… P-papa…" the frail voice cried. "It's m-me, Beth. P-please… help me… I want to go home."

"Where are you, Beth?" William said, making his way along the deck, straining to see the child in the shadowed darkness. "My name is William. I'm here to help you."

"I-I don't know where I am… It's so dark… I'm s-scared," the little girl returned, louder but still somewhat muffled.

William kept moving along the rain-swept deck. "Keep talking to me, Beth, and I'll find you. I promise I'll take you home.

Tell me about your mama and papa." The voice sounded like it was coming from farther away, where several barrels had been lashed together.

After a moment, the child began to talk. "Mama likes to sing when she braids my hair. Papa always says she sounds like an angel. Mama's cheeks turn rosy when Papa says that, and then he kisses her on her rosy cheeks and that makes her giggle, and then I start giggling too and then we all giggle, even Papa..."

Smiling at the little girl's sweet description of her parents, William was able to pinpoint her voice to one of the barrels. Sliding his dirk from his boot, he used it to pry off the lid, uncovering a small child of maybe four or five years squatting in the bottom, clutching a rag doll. He snatched her up and held her tight, bracing himself against the sway of the boat. "Beth, I've got you. I've got you." He hugged her tight as the little girl burst into tears.

"Are you William?"

"Yes, sweetheart. You are a very brave little girl."

"I am?"

"Yes, indeed. I'm going to get you back home to your mama and papa, all right?"

She nodded, her wide, luminous eyes gazing up at him trustingly.

"Sweetheart... do you know your last—your other name?"

"Mama calls me Beth Ann Wilson wh-when I feed Whiskers from the breakfast table," she whimpered, clutching her dolly.

"Beth, what's your dolly's name?" he asked gently.

The little girl glanced down at her doll. "Alice."

"I didn't think there was another child, sir," Lieutenant Franklin said, running up to William.

"Lieutenant Franklin, this is Beth and her doll, Alice," William said.

The young lieutenant smiled at the child, who cuddled closer to William and gripped his shirt tightly.

"Beth?" Franklin said in a low voice. "Could she be Lord

Wilson's daughter, sir?

"Aye," William said. He knew that the child had been stolen from Hyde Park while out with her nanny. Wilson's wife had taken to her bed after the incident and had remained in a terrible state of distress since then.

William hurried to the side of the ship, where he handed the child to Franklin, who gently transferred the exhausted child into the arms of Corporal Smythe, another officer on their ship.

Looking around, the younger man added, "I thought I heard a man's cry for help."

"Yes. I suppose you did," William said in a grim voice, noticing the bobbing head had disappeared. He had forgotten about rescuing Blackstone from drowning after he heard the child crying. "A wave washed Blackstone overboard while he was trying to escape. I had hoped that we could have arrested him, questioned him, and gotten the truth from him. Unfortunately, Mother Nature claimed him instead of Lady Justice."

William had been working for the past five years to stop child-smuggling rings. They'd recovered hundreds of missing children. And while he knew they couldn't catch all the smugglers in the ring, nor did they know who their leader was, at least they'd stopped Blackstone.

William scanned the dark, choppy waves. The seas had claimed another to a watery grave. *Good riddance.*

CHAPTER ONE

London, England
September 1819

"I'VE ENJOYED MY work with the Crown, but it's been a year since I inherited the title of Viscount Dudley, and I have responsibilities I can no longer put off," William said, sipping his brandy, sitting across from his friend Lucas in his study.

Lucas and his wife, Harriett Pemberton, the Duke and Duchess of Dorman, had invited William to stay at their townhouse, but he had declined. However, he thanked his dear friends for their most welcoming gesture. There were several loose ends on his final assignments he needed to tie up before he left for the country, and he needed his study and the solitude his townhouse offered before heading to the estate.

The duchess, formerly known as Viscountess Dudley, had been compelled by her father to marry the former viscount, breaking off her engagement to Lord Lucas Pemberton. During his initial visit to the Dudley home, after being named the new Viscount Dudley, William had discovered extortion papers in his distant cousin's study, revealing that Harriett's father had forced her to abandon her engagement to Lucas and marry William's distant cousin, a man notorious for his cruelty, especially toward women. By returning the papers to Harriett, William freed her from the threats her former mother-in-law had made to grasp the money that Harriett had inherited from her late husband. A lasting friendship had formed between William, the duchess, and her new husband, the duke.

"My duchess will be most displeased when she returns and discovers you haven't tried one of Mrs. Bodin's special lemon bars. Harriett had them prepared just for you," Dorman said with a grin.

"I certainly don't want to upset your lovely wife." William smiled as he reached for one of the bars. He greatly admired his friends for their generous charitable works. Harriett also spent one day a week at the London Children's Orphanage, a home the Dormans helped fund, assisting with the children as well as helping to find good families to adopt the orphans.

"These are delicious," William said, polishing off a second bar. "I'll have my cook bake some for Michael—that is, if your cook is willing to share her recipe. My cook, Mrs. Bradberry, is one of the few servants I didn't replace, but she is still new to me, and I'm not sure she'd know this recipe."

"Of course, our cook would be happy to include a copy. In addition, I'll ask Mrs. Bodin to pack up a basket and send it along for young Michael," the duke offered.

"Thank you, I appreciate that." William's little brother, Michael, who was just eight years old, would enjoy the treats.

William was looking forward to seeing his brother again. He planned to take him to Cliffton Abbey in Dover. When their mother had succumbed to scarlet fever, during what was deemed an epidemic almost three years ago, William had been away working for the Crown. He'd become an agent with a special mandate after the war, tracking down smugglers who kidnapped children to sell on the black market. Unfortunately, Michael had been moved from one distant relative to another in the past two years. William had felt enormous guilt for not providing his brother with a stable home, especially considering his previous mission had focused on rescuing children.

"How is young Michael?" Dorman asked. "I hear he's a clever lad with a penchant for rescuing all sorts of creatures."

William chuckled. "Yes, he has a good heart. Unfortunately, not all our relatives appreciate his love of animals."

"Well, I am certain your brother will grow up to be as good a man as you are."

"Thank you, I appreciate your vote of confidence," William said. "That's one of the reasons why I want Michael to live with me. I realize how much he needs me. I am the only one left to ensure Michael has a decent upbringing, so I'm stepping back from active duty."

"The Crown will be losing a valuable man, but Michael will be gaining your fine guidance," the duke mused, refilling both brandy glasses.

William nodded his thanks. "I'm not completely leaving—not just yet. I spoke with Colonel Harrison at headquarters this morning and he asked me to stay on in a more administrative capacity." He was skilled at decoding intercepted messages by smugglers and had been asked by Harrison to take charge of that key area. It wouldn't be forever, and it would enable him to be there for Michael while tending to his duties and obligations of his title.

The door opened, and the duchess glided gracefully into the library wearing a violet-colored gown that complemented her rich, dark hair. The duke's eyes glowed as he kissed his beautiful wife on the cheek.

"I apologize for my lateness," she said with a sigh. "We had an outbreak of hair pulling and doll hiding at the orphanage." The men chuckled at her quip. "Did I miss anything?"

"No, my dear. We were just catching up on things," Dorman said, lovingly smiling at his wife as she took the seat next to him.

A maid entered a few moments later, pushing a tea cart with a platter of sandwiches and a selection of sweets, including another plate of lemon bars. As the duchess poured and the maid assisted with plating, William looked around the room, eyeing the elegant drapes adorning the tall, beveled windows, the thick Aubusson carpet, and the leather furniture. He liked the various blues and greens that the duchess had chosen to use throughout the rooms, as well as her taste in fabrics for the drapes and furnishings.

"Harriett, my compliments on the changes you implemented to the townhouse." He turned to the duke. "Dorman, is there any chance I could borrow your lovely wife to help me decorate the manor house in Kent?"

"Not a chance. Get your own wife! I love having Harriett by my side," Dorman teased. "She is talented at everything she undertakes." He winked at his blushing wife. "However, there may be another option. We haven't been to Kent in a long time, and I have a business matter that may require travel to the area."

"I would consider it an honor to help with your estate, William," Harriett said. "Perhaps we could follow once you've settled yourself. We would be happy to have Michael stay here with us while you get things sorted at your estate. We have plenty of room. The girls have an excellent governess, and Cat and Bea love animals as much as Michael does." She giggled.

William smiled. Catherine and Beatrice were Lucas and Harriett's wards, children Lucas had taken in when their parents died. It seemed his brother's penchant for rescuing wild creatures had made the rounds. "That is most kind of you. I appreciate your invitation to have Michael stay here," he said. "However, I think it would be good for my brother to live with me at Cliffton Abbey. It would be good for me as well." Even though William would be immersed in the estate business, he would have plenty of time to spend with Michael.

"Our friendship is something I never anticipated," Harriett mused before she sipped her tea. "I ignored every effort you initially made to contact me, thinking you would be the horrid person my former mother-in-law described. As awful as my late husband was, she made no bones about wanting everything her son had left to me—she didn't feel I should've received even a farthing."

"Well, I'm glad she didn't get her way," William said, his tone firm. He had made certain of that himself, instructing his capable staff—including Franklin, who had remained loyal to him, as well as his newly appointed butler and housekeeper—to ensure the old harridan was gone from Cliffton Abbey well before his arrival.

William had understood Harriett's dilemma the moment he spoke to Harriett's former mother-in-law, and when he discovered the extortion papers that the late viscount had used to marry Harriett, he had had a fairly good idea of what had transpired.

He shook his head. "But as horrible as the whole affair was, had I not inherited his title—something I never anticipated—I would have never met you or your husband, and two finer friends I have never had," William said. "And I cannot disagree that the title has given me an advantage that is much appreciated where my brother is concerned."

"I couldn't agree more," Lucas added, lifting his brandy glass in a toast. "Harriett has returned to me as my wife, and my life is all the richer and happier for it. William, your friendship is a gift as well. Let me speak with my man of affairs, and I'll update you on our possible travel to Cliffton Abbey."

"I should give fair warning. The latest report from my man of business revealed the manor house needs much repair," William said. "This will be my first time living there."

Harriett harumphed. "I wish *I* had never lived there," she said tightly, her voice trembling with anger—and no doubt the painful memories of having essentially been a prisoner there.

Dorman wrapped his arm around his wife's slender shoulders and hugged her close.

"There is a decent central living area, but the older wings need significant refurbishment and repair," the duchess said, sounding calmer. "I would be happy to make suggestions. I would like nothing more than to see it transformed into a bright and welcoming place to live." She paused. "There was also a tunnel that wound down to the beach. I must show you where it is—but my understanding is that tunnels run throughout the property and possibly connect to the estate it borders. I never mentioned it to your cousin, but it was the only way I had any semblance of freedom, where I didn't feel spied upon. I used it every chance I got. I discovered it by accident and realized his servants didn't seem aware of it."

William couldn't imagine how difficult that must have been for Harriett—living in near isolation while her every move was watched and reported on. Nothing about his cousin had surprised him; he had been a cold, unscrupulous man. William would have to do his utmost to change the perception people had of the title of Viscount Dudley. Each time he was introduced with his new title, people eyed him speculatively until they were sure he was not of the same ilk as the late viscount.

"Thank you. Knowledge of a tunnel would be an important piece of information, especially if I'm to have a very adventurous eight-year-old with me," William said with a laugh. "Michael's favorite pastime is playing pirate, when he's not rescuing stray animals. Finding a secret passage to the sandy beaches of Dover would be perfect for him. I'll need to look into that."

The duke chuckled. "A secret tunnel is a definite draw for children. Certainly, something we would love to have discovered when we were that age."

"A boy with Michael's spirit will certainly offer a hearty challenge," Harriett added. "Perhaps I could be of assistance in securing you a governess. It might make things easier."

William was glad she didn't echo Dorman's teasing him about getting a wife. He had no immediate plans to marry. Despite his having acquired the title of a man who was greatly disliked, word of William's missions had spread among the *ton*. He'd become recognized as a hero of sorts, and at every ball or dinner he'd been forced to attend, he'd found himself avoiding all the young debutantes. He had hoped to divest himself of the Crown's responsibilities and remove himself from London, where people in his set lauded him at every turn for saving the lives of children who'd been stolen and bound for slavery—among them, a child of a fellow peer.

If he were being honest with himself, he'd admit that he'd enjoyed the work—the connection with his team, the common purpose.

It was the same feeling he'd had when he was in the army. What his admirers didn't know was that while William had let the man who committed the crime drown, he now understood he hadn't gotten the head of the snake. However, he hadn't lost any sleep over Blackstone's dying. Rescuing Beth Ann Wilson and returning her to her loving parents had been worth it. The death of that bastard Blackstone was still a win. If that made William more ruthless and less heroic, so be it. The problem was—he hadn't put an end to the Pied Piper. The villain was still out there.

CHAPTER TWO

Three weeks later
Bridgewater Manor
Dover, Kent

"LACEY… WHERE ARE you?" Lady Bella Connolly called to her dog. Lacey never wandered away. Bella had swung open the kitchen door five minutes ago, the savory scent of beef stew and warm bread from their midday meal lingering behind her, and let Lacey out, trusting her faithful companion to play in the familiar, grassy expanse as she always did. Now, as Bella stepped outside, wrapping her shawl around her shoulders to ward off the biting cold, a sense of unease washed over her. The yard was usually noisy from Lacey's exuberant barking and her penchant for digging up flowers, but the area felt unsettlingly quiet.

"Come on, Lacey, where are you?" Bella called. She put two fingers under her tongue and gave a loud whistle for her dog—something her father had taught her, although her Uncle Stephen often chided her for such an unladylike display.

"Come on, girl. The weather's too cold for you. Where are you?" Bella called again, but saw no movement anywhere. She looked anxiously at the dark cluster of clouds above her. Worry seeped into her as she searched the area around the house for Lacey's familiar shape, but she saw nothing. Lacey had disappeared.

A moment later, Bella heard a whimper that sounded like Lacey, and she hurried in the direction of the sound, on her father's property—*correction*, her Uncle Stephen's property. Her chest tightened with the grief that had become a part of her life since her father's death, nearly a year ago, leaving her alone. Oh, she had Grandmère—her mother's mother—who had been by her side since her mother's untimely death from the wasting disease two years ago. And she had Grandmama, her father's mother. The two of them had become great friends over the years, and now that they were both widows, they were more like sisters than extended family.

But except for her grandmothers and Lacey, Bella had no other family. Uncle Stephen—her father's younger brother—didn't quite count. While he was her guardian, he'd made it painfully clear that she was a *loose end* for him—a guardianship he felt forced to assume unless he wanted the scorn that would come from denying her a home and his oversight. Her uncle used to be fun and jovial—someone that, as a little girl, Bella had loved to spend time with—but since he had returned from the Napoleonic Wars, he had been sullen and difficult. He detested spending time with anyone.

As she searched the shrubs that lined the property, Bella recalled the horrible arguments between her father and his brother, often in the middle of the night, so loud they woke her. With her bedroom above her father's study and their voices so loud, Bella had heard every word. Uncle Stephen would show up on their doorstep, demanding money to cover various "legitimate expenses," which her father knew very well were gaming debts or money to pay for his love of wining and dining actresses or dancers around town. As she thought about it, she realized that for at least the last ten years, she couldn't recall her uncle spending any time with her family. Except for those late-night visits. Uncle Stephen had been a virtual stranger until he'd become her guardian.

Usually, Papa would admonish his brother and pay the debts.

But a month before her father's death, they'd had a very bitter fight, and she heard Papa tell Uncle Stephen he would no longer pay his debts, that his monthly allowance was more than enough to cover his expenses, and to take responsibility like a man. Uncle Stephen told Papa that he would regret that decision and slammed the door. She remembered feeling the same sense of unease as she felt now.

A few short weeks later, Papa was gone. He had broken his neck while riding his horse. It had been a complete and utter shock. Her father was an expert horseman, and Winterborne was his favorite horse. She loved the horse, too, and realized she hadn't ridden it in almost a year. She still visited Winterborne in his stall, but one of the grooms took on the duty of exercising him. Not because she was angry at the beloved animal, but because Winterborne had not only been her father's horse, he'd also been his best friend.

Since that day, Winterborne had never been the same. The horse had become quiet and almost afraid of venturing out too far. Bella was worried about him and knew that something needed to be done to somehow coax the animal from his dejected state of mind. Bella could certainly understand Winterborne's sadness, for she felt it too. Her whole life had changed that day as well.

Not only had she lost her biggest supporter, she'd lost the one person she could share her hopes and fears with, her dreams for the future. But now she had a stranger as a guardian. A man she barely knew had replaced the man she adored more than anyone. Her new guardian had moved her and her grandmothers to the summer house in Dover, Kent, for fresh air and brisk walks to alleviate her grief.

Bella hadn't wanted the fresh air of Dover. She missed her home, missed sitting in her father's study, in his great leather armchair surrounded by his books and his tobacco, and the portrait of her father and late mother that hung over the fireplace mantel. She needed familiarity, and her parents had purchased this home two years ago. Mama had accompanied them the summer of that first year. But it was only Papa and Bella who came in the second year. That was last year when Papa died. As far as Bella was concerned, *this wasn't her home.*

But Bella's voice meant little. Uncle Stephen was now in charge.

"Lacey, I have treats for you, girl," she called, praying she'd hear her dog's whimpers again. So intent was she on the memories of her late father and her missing dog that Bella neglected to be mindful of where she was walking. By the time the thought occurred to her, she realized she'd wandered onto the neighbor's land. She had never even met her neighbor, Viscount Dudley, who hadn't lived here until this year. *No matter. As soon as I find Lacey, I'll hurry back.*

"Lacey, girl. Where are you?" she called out again. "I have treats. Treats, Lacey! Treats!" She said it in a singsong voice, over and over.

She heard Lacey's bark. *Finally!* The lure of treats had done the trick. From its sound, Bella thought the dog was nearby. It was cold, and she wanted nothing more than to return home to the warmth of the kitchen. The Dover house was nice in the summer, but it could turn frigid this time of year, especially so close to the edge of the cliffs.

The mighty waves of the English Channel connecting to the North Sea via the Strait of Dover reverberated against the cliffs. Despite the chill in the air, the view was breathtaking, and Bella made a mental note to visit this lovely spot again on a warmer day. She would find a sunny patch of grass and tuck into a captivating book. She paused long enough to appreciate the view but, noticing the clouds darkening, soon returned to the task at hand. The whimpering grew louder. As Lacey followed the sound of her dog, she poked through the different grasses and wildflowers that lined the cliff's edge, and the roar of the waves below grew much louder. Hearing another bark, Bella realized that Lacey sounded closer.

Methodically, she pushed her way through the tall grasses and crouched low between the bushes, looking beneath and behind them for her dog. The animal's whimpers and barking grew louder. "Lacey, I hear you. Where are you, you mischievous dog?"

As Bella neared the next bush, her foot landed on loose ground, and she slipped. Letting out a shrill cry, she slid over the edge, desperately reaching for anything to grip to keep from falling over the cliff. A sob of relief escaped her as her hand tangled in a clump of thick weeds. Bella frantically hung on for dear life, admonishing herself for becoming distracted by her thoughts.

From above, she could hear Lacey's yipping. She glanced up and saw her dog peering over the edge.

"Lacey, get help," she cried.

The dog barked frantically as it darted back and forth from the cliff's edge as if urging her to hold on tight.

Bella closed her eyes, praying she had the strength to hold on to the roots and wishing someone would come to her rescue. But all she had was Lacey—and despite Lacey's being a clever animal, she feared there was little the dog could do. She glanced around, searching for anything that could help her. Her skirts and petticoats were weighing her down, and her arms were becoming numb.

She heard the bushes above rustle again after what seemed like the longest few minutes of her life. "Lacey, please get help," she pleaded. "Tell someone that I'm here. Find Uncle—"

"I'm here to help," a deep voice said from above her, as a man with wavy blond hair and deep-blue eyes leaned over the edge. "There are some protruding roots just to the right of your feet. If you move your right foot, you will feel them. They'll help you stay balanced."

She did as he instructed, and her feet found the roots. They were still flimsy, but he was right. They gave her something to balance on.

"Th-thank you, sir." Bella nodded, unsure how long she could hold on.

A few moments later she heard his voice from somewhere below her, which only confused her more. "I want you to trust me—what's your name?"

"B-Bella."

"Bella, I'm William. I'm standing below you and just to your right."

"H-how can you be…?"

"There's a ledge beneath you—about ten feet below your feet. I found a path to take me down here."

"I-I'm sorry. I didn't see the ledge."

"That's all right, Bella. I'm going to catch you. But you must promise to do exactly as I say."

"Y-yes, sir."

"Good girl, Bella. When I say let go, I want you to let go and just let yourself drop." He must have noticed her stiffen at his instruction because he added, "This ledge is wide enough and sturdy enough to hold us both."

"Are you certain?"

"I'm certain, Bella," he said in a deep, calm voice.

Lacey barked wildly as if she were telling Bella to trust him.

"I do, girl," she said, her voice faint. "But I can't hold on much longer."

"You don't need to. I'm here," the soothing male voice said below her. "I'm going to catch you."

Bella's heart pounded as she clung to the ledge, too terrified to look down. "You promise to catch me?"

"Yes, I promise. Trust me. I'm right here. Just let go," he murmured, voice steady and sure.

Her fingers ached, frozen stiff, and unresponsive, as if they no longer belonged to her. She squeezed her eyes shut, whispered a desperate prayer, and released her grip.

For an instant, she was weightless. The wind roared past her, pulling her downward. The jagged rocks below seemed to reach up, hungry and waiting. A scream tore from her throat, sharp and involuntary—

But then she stopped falling.

Strong arms wrapped around her, solid and unyielding.

"I've got you, Bella. I've got you," he rasped, his voice rough with exertion.

The impact of her fall must have jolted him, and for a harrowing moment, his footing slipped. Her panic surged, and she let out a frantic yelp, flailing against him.

Then there was a thud—a hard, jolting stop.

Bella lay still, gasping for breath, her senses spinning. Was she alive? The air felt too rich, too vibrant to belong to Heaven. A warm, grounding presence surrounded her—sandalwood, citrus, and leather mingled with the sea's salt.

She stirred, feeling the solid heat of his body beneath her. Slowly, she opened her eyes, and the world came into focus: not the endless blue of sky or water, but the deepest, most mesmerizing blue she'd ever seen. Her rescuer's eyes.

He lay beneath her, chest heaving, his arms still holding her securely.

"You're safe," he murmured, his breath brushing her cheek.

For the first time since the fall, she believed him.

"I'm on top of you." She felt silly stating the obvious. But it was as much in wonderment as anything else. "You saved me."

"I suppose I did," he said with a husky laugh.

His laugh seemed to rumble from deep in his chest. It was the nicest sound she'd ever heard.

Lacey came racing down a small turn onto the cliff, skidded next to her, and licked her face. "Lacey, I want to be mad at you, but I'm too relieved at not being dead," Bella finally said, moving her head away from her dog's tongue as soon as she stopped licking. "Thank you... William."

"You're welcome... Bella."

She couldn't stop staring into his eyes. And then she realized she was still lying on top of him. On top of his big, muscular frame.

"I'm lying on top of you," she blurted.

"Yes, you are." His eyes twinkled.

Lord, he's handsome. How in the world did this handsome stranger happen along and save her life? His golden, wavy hair and blue eyes made her wonder if he was an angel sent from Heaven.

"Are you real?"

He laughed. "Yes, Bella, I assure you, I am very real."

That rumbling laugh made her heart do a million flip-flops in her chest.

"I have a suggestion," he said.

"Yes?" She couldn't stop gazing into his eyes.

"Perhaps we should get up and get back to sturdy ground?"

"Oh, y-yes… Yes, of course."

"Let me help you," he said as he gently lifted her off him.

She winced as her sore hands touched the ground beneath her.

"Are you hurt?" he asked.

"Just my hands are a bit scraped."

"We'll get you some salve, but in the meantime, we need to get you back home."

He helped her stand and kept his hands on her waist as she wobbled.

"I've always been in love with Dover, but this wasn't the way I had envisioned seeing the White Cliffs." It was a feeble attempt at humor, she realized, but it was what she did when she was nervous.

"Hopefully, the rest of your visit will be better."

"Yes, hopefully." She smiled.

"Allow me to introduce myself more formally. I am Viscount William Dudley. I have but recently inherited this estate and, quite truthfully, only just arrived. I was acquainting myself with the grounds when your dog approached with rather impressive urgency, compelling me to follow her."

Lacey barked as though confirming what he'd said.

"I am grateful for what you did for me today," Bella said, feeling his steadying hand as she trembled anew. "I am Lady Bella Connolly. My father... I mean, my family owns Bridgewater Manor, the pink stone and limestone manor next to your estate. My father recently died, and Uncle Stephen brought me and my grandmothers here... with Lacey, of course."

"A pleasure to make your acquaintance," he said, dipping his head in a subtle bow.

She sighed softly at the sound of his voice. It was rich and smooth, with a cadence that made her feel as though she were being invited to dance at a grand London ball during the height of the Season.

He pointed his chin at Lacey. "She's a beautiful dog. Quite precocious and with a knack for getting into scrapes, it seems. I spotted her earlier sniffing at an animal trap someone had left ready to spring. Reacting, I threw a rock on the trap and sprang it before it could grab her."

Lacey gave a soft woof and wagged her tail.

"Lacey," Bella gently admonished her. She felt her face heat with a blush. "It's not like her to get into scrapes, truly. But it was my fault. I shouldn't have let her out on her own. She is most curious, and I expect she was excited to explore."

"Don't be too hard on her. You're fortunate to have such a clever dog. She found me as I was clearing part of a stone wall that had crumbled and frantically barked at me to follow her." He reached down and petted the black dog, who responded by licking his hand. "I like you too, Lacey."

"Lacey rarely likes men, except for my father—my late father," Bella said, amazed at her dog's affection for the stranger.

"Well, it wasn't our first meeting," he said. "A sudden rain shower forced me to seek shelter while walking my land yesterday, so I ran into an empty shed—probably an old groundskeeper's shed. I thought I noticed her watching me from the cover of some trees, but I left her alone."

"Interesting. That must have been in the morning. I ended up in our stables watching the rain. She must have heard you and slipped outside to have a peek," Bella said, giving a slight smile.

He held her arm as he escorted her up the narrow path back to higher ground and to her manor house, with Lacey trotting in front, leading the way.

They walked for a good fifteen or twenty minutes. Bella hadn't realized how deep onto his property she had gone. She'd need to use Lacey's leash in the future if the dog was going to continue running off. She'd had the dog since she was a puppy, and now that Lacey was two, she wasn't as rambunctious and was less inclined to disobey, usually. Bella shuddered at the thought of the trap. "Do you trap animals on your property… Lord Dudley?"

"No, I don't. And please, I fear we've met in the unlikeliest of places. Call me William," he said. "I've only recently become a viscount, so I am unused to this formality. But we were discussing the trap. I admit, it was a shock to discover it, and I don't condone those traps. I need to investigate and make certain there are no others. I wouldn't want anyone to be injured—horse or a person… or your brave Lacey."

As they reached the front door of her home, Bella turned to William. "Would you come for tea tomorrow?" she asked. "As a proper thank you. And my grandmothers, Grandmama and Grandmère, would love to meet you."

"I'd be honored," William replied. "Though I should mention that my younger brother, Michael, will be arriving tomorrow morning. He's eight years old. Would you mind if I brought him along?"

"Of course not. We would love to meet your brother."

Bella smiled up at him. But as she spoke, William blinked at her, his expression shifting, as though she were some new enigma he hadn't quite figured out.

"Would two o'clock be a good time for you and Michael?" she asked.

"Two it is," he answered, wearing a warm smile.

"Thank you again for saving me, Lord Dudley," she said softly.

"William," he corrected her gently.

"William," she repeated, the name feeling familiar and comforting on her lips.

"You're welcome, Bella," he said.

CHAPTER THREE

The next day
Cliffton Abbey
Dover, England

THESE TRANQUIL WALKS at dawn had the potential to be a cherished routine, William mused as he found himself pausing at the spot where Lady Bella Connolly had slipped down the cliff. He leaned over the edge, scanning the sandy ledge where he had caught her and where the faint imprint of their footprints still lingered. A wave of gratitude washed over him, his heart swelling as he recalled the adrenaline of yesterday's close call.

Bella was, without a doubt, the most vivacious and enchanting young woman he had ever encountered. The mere thought that he'd see her later today filled him with an anticipatory warmth. William couldn't recall when a woman had captivated his attention so completely. But an exhilarating spark in her playful spirit made him want to uncover more layers of her personality.

His mind drifted deeper into contemplation, and he became momentarily lost in the memory of her laughter and the light in her eyes.

As a gentle breeze stirred the air, a delicate trace of jasmine drifted past him—her scent, light and sweet, as if she had just been there. The fleeting fragrance startled him, and he looked at his surroundings, half expecting to find her standing nearby. But reality settled in a moment later—he was alone.

Then movement off in the distance caught his eye. As he strained against the brightness of the rising sun, he thought he saw a ship. He'd been here almost three weeks and hadn't seen a single vessel. Quickly, he slid his spyglass from the holster on his belt and directed it at the ship. The boat didn't appear to be moving.

With the spyglass, he could make out a small dinghy being rowed out over the crest of the waves to meet it. He shifted his view to the flag being hauled to the top of the mast, hoping he might recognize some kind of identity. But whoever was manning the vessel was flying it under a flag he'd never seen before. It certainly wasn't the Union Jack, nor was it one of the merchant ships. Considering the time of day, this all felt suspicious. Taking a seat on a nearby rock, he withdrew a small sketchbook and drew the flag's symbol.

Afterward, he made his way back to the manor, moving through the trees to avoid drawing the attention of whoever was manning the boat. Once he was back at the house, he hurried to his study to send a missive with his drawing to Colonel Harrison. He tugged on the shabby brown velvet cord near his desk. The door to his study immediately opened, and Harlow entered. William noticed how quickly Harlow always responded and fleetingly wondered if the man camped outside the door, waiting to be summoned.

"Yes, my lord?" Harlow said.

"Have Franklin see that this is delivered to Colonel Harrison's office in London." Before being hired by William, Harlow had retired from many faithful years of service with the Crown. William had also hired Franklin officially as a footman, but the young man had been one of the Crown's most trusted messengers and continued to work with him in that capacity. "In addition, my younger brother should arrive this morning, and we have an invitation to meet the neighbors, Lady Connolly and her grandmothers... Er... I don't seem to recall her giving me either of her grandmothers' names." He had been too distracted by the events, he assumed.

"If you will allow me, my lord," Harlow said. "I may be able to help with the names. I had the pleasure of assisting the grand ladies when they stopped in town on their arrival several weeks ago. The shorter lady with gray hair is the Dowager Viscountess Elise Harrington. Her husband was the late Viscount Phillip Harrington. And the taller one is the Dowager Countess Anna Bridgewater. Lovely ladies, if I say so myself."

The older man quickly stepped back, his face a mottled red. William had never seen Harlow embarrassed and momentarily turned his face away from the man to hide the smile that overtook his face.

Harlow handed him a missive from the Duke of Dorman and a carefully wrapped package. "They arrived with this morning's mail, my lord," he said.

William opened the package. "Excellent. Michael and I can bring some of these to tea at Bridgewater Manor this afternoon. Would you ask Mrs. Bradberry to find a decorative tin for them?"

"No trouble at all, my lord. You mentioned the tea was at two. I'll have the tin ready for you."

"Thank you, Harlow," William said, his voice full of gratitude.

"You are most welcome, my lord." With a swift bow, Harlow left the room.

A few minutes later, William finished reading the letter from Dorman and, setting it down on his desk, leaned back in his chair. Dorman had written to say their visit would possibly be delayed by a week or two.

It would be good to see the duke and duchess again. William hadn't realized how much he enjoyed social activities with friends until he left London for Kent. He was staying busy, and normally, he enjoyed the solitude to focus on his work, but the isolation of Dover had begun to wear on him.

Until yesterday. Meeting the lovely Lady Bella Connolly—

despite the foul weather that rolled in the moment he'd returned home—had made his day. She had made an impression on him—so much so that he found himself thinking of her every spare moment. He needed to stop doing so. He wasn't looking for a relationship—there wasn't time for that. He needed to get Michael settled.

There was too much to do and no time for love or romantic entanglements—at least, not now.

His lips twitched with amusement as he recalled Lucas's remark when he'd casually mentioned Harriett's help with decorating. Dorman had chuckled and suggested that William ought to find a wife of his own.

He had brushed off the comment at the time, but deep down, he couldn't ignore the quiet pang of envy at the closeness Harriett and Lucas shared. Of course, he wanted that kind of love—one day.

But not now.

His internal reasoning should have settled the matter. However, it didn't. His mind wandered back to yesterday… to Bella… Her lush curves and her beautiful golden hair. Her captivating jasmine scent.

Focus, man! Stop thinking about that pretty girl. You have a hundred and one things to do.

He'd been anxious about his arrival. He was relieved that his London staff had willingly agreed to accompany him. They'd left a skeleton staff in London—just a handful of trusted individuals to oversee the townhouse and ensure everything ran smoothly in his absence. It wasn't a question of financial consideration; his cousin had amassed a considerable fortune, and William could easily afford more help. Instead, his decision stemmed from the immediacy of the current situation, requiring a full complement of staff at the country house instead of the city residence.

In the drawing room, Mr. Harlow and Mrs. Aberdeen had already begun interviewing additional personnel for the Kent home. They had begun assessing candidates to fill roles from kitchen staff to groundskeepers, aiming to create a cohesive team that would ensure the house was both welcoming and efficiently managed. Time was of the essence, and William knew that securing the right staff was crucial. He was very appreciative to have a butler of Mr. Harlow's temperament and background, as well as his housekeeper, Mrs. Aberdeen.

A tap sounded and Harlow stepped into the room.

"My lord, the kitchen staff found this lovely tin for the lemon bars," he said, presenting a tastefully decorated tin.

"Perfect," William said.

"Very good, my lord. I shall make sure you have it when you are ready to leave."

"By the way, Harlow," William said, "the Duke and Duchess of Dorman plan to visit in two weeks. Her Grace has agreed to help us with refurbishing the manor. Ask Mrs. Aberdeen to have the nursery readied, in case they bring the children and their governess."

"I'll inform Mrs. Aberdeen, your lordship. And may I add, you've made an excellent choice? The duchess has already earned a remarkable reputation among the *ton* for her decorating talent."

"Thank you for that, too. I'm new to this, as you know. I appreciate any thoughts or insight you can provide."

Harlow acknowledged the compliment with a nod and a bow before he left.

Since he still had a few hours before he needed to be at Lady Connolly's for tea, William decided to investigate the area where he had found the iron trap. It could have seriously maimed an animal—or a person, for that matter. He wanted to know what it was doing on his property. Nothing in his late cousin's papers mentioned trapping or providing permission to trappers.

As odd as it seemed to him, the former viscount had been generous to several animal charities—based on his ledgers. So, it was strange that he had given to such charities and at the same time approved trapping on his land. The late viscount had had many egregious faults, but cruelty to animals didn't seem to be among them. One charity was a local farm that took on wounded animals and rehabilitated them. William shook his head when he thought about that.

He'd have to ask Harriett about it when she and Lucas arrived. The duchess could surely shed some light on that. In the meantime, he'd do the best he could to locate who the trapper was, or if there were others. He'd given the trap to his newly hired groundskeeper, who assured him he would find out who had made the trap or where it had been purchased. Like his footman and butler, his groundskeeper worked both for the Crown and William. No one else was aware of the dual employment outside of those four.

A half-hour later, he found Mr. Pickens in the garden. "Were you able to tell anything from the trap?" he asked.

Mr. Pickens stood. "Your lordship. I didn't identify the person, but I may have found out where they were purchased. The local blacksmith, Mr. Embers. I tried to find him while I was in town, but he was not at the smithy. His wife said he'd gone to a neighboring village for supplies."

"That's good information. Do you think he'll give you the name?" William asked.

"Depends, my lord. I know the smithy. If the person who ordered the traps didn't want his name given and threatened him to keep that quiet, or wore a disguise, then no."

"Thank you for looking into it, Pickens. Perhaps I will give the local farrier a visit," William said. He certainly wasn't above passing a coin or two to discover the origin of the traps.

Pickens gave a small bow before continuing to prune the rosebushes. "I'll have these gardens in shape for spring soon, sir."

"You've made a significant change in the few days we've been here. Carry on, Mr. Pickens."

An hour later, William returned to his study to make some notes. He had located two more traps—one had been sprung, but the animal had managed to escape. He'd sprung the other. A betting man would put money on there being more traps, he thought angrily. He'd speak to Harlow and Pickens about organizing a small posse of footmen and stable hands to scour the rest of the land. He wanted the traps removed.

Curiously, each trap was close to where he had found the first one—near the edge of the cliff, where he had helped Lady Bella Connolly. William also planned to set up security around the perimeter of his property. He wanted to know who was placing the traps... and why.

Harlow tapped on the door and entered, holding a tin of lemon bars. "I promised to make sure you had this before you left. I believe this will be perfect for your invitation to tea, my lord. It rivals any container of sweets the emporium in town could offer and looks as good as anything I saw in London."

"That should work out quite well. By the way, I mentioned discovering an iron trap yesterday while walking the property. Today, I found two more. One had already been sprung—thankfully, nothing seemed to have been caught. The other, I triggered with a rock. Please assemble a small group of men—including Pickens and several footmen, men you believe would do a thorough job—and have them walk the entire property. We need to locate any remaining traps and get rid of them. They are dangerous."

"I'll be happy to do that, my lord," Harlow replied. "I'll do so right away."

"And tell the men not to discuss it with anyone. I mean it. I don't want to alert the person who set the traps or anyone working with him—just in case they're from around here or the village. I'd prefer we smoke him out and confront him."

"I understand, my lord. We will mobilize and check the land," Harlow said.

"The land surrounding the manor first," William added.

"Of course, my lord." With that, Harlow left.

William settled back in his desk chair and spun around to the large window behind his desk. His little brother would want to go riding, or at the very least, learn how to ride. He could think of so many reasons to discover who had set these traps and make sure they never set another on his property. They were ghoulish creations, designed to maim and torture.

Closing his eyes, he summoned the vivid image of Lady Connolly—an apparition he had deliberately avoided all afternoon by immersing himself in work. He could still feel the cold grip of fear that had washed over him the moment he saw her dangling from the protruding roots of the cliff. And he felt a surge of gratitude for the narrow ledge that had provided her a lifeline. Somehow, she had managed to grip those roots, breaking her fall. He could only imagine the fear and was thankful for the ledge; otherwise, he didn't know how he would have saved her in time to prevent disaster.

A smile crept onto his face as he thought about her spirit. Once she had regained her composure, shaken but unbroken, she displayed remarkable calm. Instead of dwelling on the harrowing experience, she'd expressed her gratitude and invited him to tea. Even as he escorted her home, her demeanor had been sweet and shy, but with good humor in the depths of her luminous green eyes; there had been no dramatic outbursts. Exactly the opposite of what he had experienced at *ton* events he had attended since attaining his title.

Damn it, man, stop thinking about her as if you intend to court her. You have far too many matters to attend to without getting sidetracked by the lovely Bella Connolly.

The door to his study opened and Harlow stepped inside. William heard a little boy shouting and running down the hall. A second later, Michael came bounding into the room. "Will, I'm heeere!" the small boy said, leaping into William's outstretched arms and throwing his small arms around his big brother.

William laughed. "Yes, I can see that. Welcome home, Michael. Welcome home!" he said, hugging his little brother and kissing him on the head.

CHAPTER FOUR

Later that day
Bridgewater Manor
Dover, Kent

"WELCOME, MY LORD. The ladies are in the drawing room," the butler said, showing William and Michael the way.

"This will be fun, won't it, Will?" Michael said, hopping from one foot to the other as they followed the butler.

"It will," William said. "Michael, remember what we talked about?"

"Oh, yes. I'm sorry," Michael said, settling immediately into a cordial walk and no longer hopping.

William smiled—the simple instruction confirmed he had influence with his brother, which would be important. He recalled the first time he'd accompanied his father and mother on a social call at that age, and he was just like Michael until his parents gave him a gentle reminder about his behavior. "And remember what I said… you can have as many biscuits as you like, but one at a time."

"Yes, Will," Michael said with a grin stretching across his face, displaying two missing teeth in the front.

William gave Michael's hand an affectionate squeeze, realizing again how glad he was to have his little brother with him.

"My ladies, Viscount William Dudley has arrived with Master

Michael Dudley," the butler announced.

Bella gracefully approached. "Lord Dudley, it's our pleasure to have you and your brother join us for tea," she said, her smile warm and welcoming.

William blinked, once again struck by her beauty—her soft green gown shimmering faintly in the afternoon light, accented her slender figure and the subtle glow of her complexion, the striking brilliance of her emerald-green eyes, and the gentle waves of her golden-blonde hair.

His attention shifted, and he noticed the faint limp in her step. A rush of protective instinct surged within him, and for an instant, he longed to sweep her up in his arms, remembering what it felt like to hold her. He quickly reprimanded himself, forcing his focus back to the moment.

"Allow me to introduce you to my grandmothers," she continued. "This is Grandmère, the Dowager Viscountess Elise Harrington."

The short, gray-haired woman gave a gentle nod and extended her hand.

William took it and bowed over it. "It's very nice to make your acquaintance, my lady."

"It's nice to meet you, my lady," Michael said, first looking up at William and then taking the viscountess's hand in his chubby one and kissing it.

"Thank you both. The pleasure is all mine," she said with a soft French accent, smiling down at Michael. "Please, I would be honored if you would call me Grandmère."

"*Gwand-mare*," Michael pronounced carefully.

Fleetingly, Bella wondered why Michael mixed up the R and W sounds; it seemed to occur whenever the young boy was excited or flustered.

"Yes, darling boy," she said graciously.

Bella's lips twitched as she started to introduce her other grandmother. "This is Grandmama, the Dowager Countess Anna Bridgewater." She nodded at the taller woman.

Before she could say anything, William's younger brother took the dowager's hand into his and kissed it. "It's a *pleasure* to meet you, Gwand-mama," he said. Then he looked up at William. "Why does Lady Bella have two gwandmothers and we don't, William?"

"Michael, that happens in some families."

"I wish *I* had a gwandmother."

"You sweet boy!" Lady Bridgewater exclaimed. "We would be pleased to be your honorary grandmothers. Isn't that so, Elise?"

"Oh, I agree wholeheartedly, Anna," the viscountess said. "Consider us your grandmothers, young Michael." She turned to her friend. "He is so charming," she whispered loudly.

Lady Bridgewater nodded. "Angelic. He reminds me of a cherub."

Bella smiled as her eyes met William's. William thought *she* looked like an angel. "Lady Bella, I'm very glad to see you looking well. How is your ankle?"

He noticed Bella blushed at the question, which made him want to talk her into his arms and kiss her.

"Much better. Thank you," she said. "I don't know what I would have done if Lacey hadn't found you. I certainly couldn't have held on too much longer."

Hearing her name, the long-haired black dog trotted into the room and immediately took position at Bella's feet.

"You have a dog?" Michael asked. "I love dogs."

"We do," Bella said while her fingers absently combed Lacey's soft hair between her ears. As she did that, the animal leaned into her affectionate ministrations.

"My goodness! If she were a cat, she'd be purring," Lady Bridgewater said. "Listen to her. She almost gives a guttural hum, just like a cat."

"Very true," her other grandmother agreed.

"Forgive me, where are my manners? I forgot to give you this. Lemon bars, baked by the cook of a dear friend," William said, handing the tin to Bella.

"Thank you, my lord," she said with a soft smile.

"Wonderful, we can enjoy them with our tea," Grandmère said, nodding at Garrett, the butler.

A minute later, a maid pushed a tea cart laden with biscuits, finger sandwiches, and tea into the room. The butler opened the tin that Bella handed him and added the lemon bars onto a plate.

"Michael, our cook, Mrs. Bisque, prepared some lemonade. Do you enjoy lemonade?" Lady Harrington asked.

"It's my favowite," the little boy said, accepting the glass and selecting one of the lemon bars. "I love them almost as much as pirates. Is that a painting of a pirate ship?" he asked with awe.

"What a sharp eye you have, Michael," Lady Harrington said. "It does look like a pirate ship, but it was painted by my son Stephen, Bella's uncle. As far as I know, it's not a specific ship. He painted it with several images in mind."

"It's jolly good," Michael said, "even if it's not a pirate ship."

"Ah, so you love pirates, yes?" Grandmère asked. "Have you ever hunted for lost treasure?"

"No, but finding tweasure is a big dream of mine!" Michael exclaimed, his voice bubbling with enthusiasm as everyone chuckled around the table.

William already knew his brother's imagination was easily captivated by tales of swashbuckling rogues and buried treasure. It was precisely the kind of topic that sparked his enthusiasm. He was heartened by the kindness of their neighbors, particularly Bella's grandmothers, who proved to be warm-hearted women with a natural affinity for children. Their evident delight in Michael's presence reassured William that bringing his eight-year-old brother to live with him had been the right decision. He had a feeling that Bella and her grandmothers would have a most positive influence on the boy.

"This is good," Michael said with his mouth full of powdered sugar. "Is there pirate treasure to find here?" Lacey's ears perked up, and she trotted over to sit at Michael's feet.

"Perhaps..." Grandmère's voice was tinged with excitement as she spoke excitedly to the small boy. "I heard a story in town that might interest you."

"Elise, perhaps we shouldn't..." Lady Bridgewater began hesitantly.

"Poppycock! I think it will be a splendid adventure," Lady Harrington declared with a twinkle in her eye.

"What sort of adventure?" Michael asked eagerly, his curiosity piqued.

"A hunt for buried treasure, *mon cher*," Lady Harrington said with dramatic flair. "They say that many, many years ago—perhaps a century or more—a pirate landed on these very shores and concealed a most precious treasure. There's an old woman in the village who knows the story in all its details."

Lady Bridgewater chuckled warmly. "Of course, we cannot be certain if it's true or merely a fanciful tale, but I happen to know someone who might. Perhaps tomorrow we can organize a small adventure, visit the village, and ask Grandmère's friend about this mysterious legend."

Michael turned to William, his eyes wide with an almost irresistible plea. "Oh, please, Will, may I go to town tomorrow with my new grandmothers?"

To strengthen his case, Michael patted Lacey on the head. The loyal dog sat up immediately, wagging her tail as though she wholeheartedly endorsed the idea. "See? Even Lacey thinks it's a good idea."

William hesitated, his gaze shifting from Bella to her grandmothers. The three women were smiling, their expressions so warm and inviting that it was difficult to refuse.

"We would be delighted to have you join us," Lady Bridgewater said with a gracious nod. "We can stop by the tea shop for chocolate and scones."

"It will also give you and Michael a chance to become acquainted with the town and meet some of the local artisans," Bella suggested with a charming smile. "Especially since you plan to refurbish your estate."

William sighed, the corner of his mouth tugging upward as he realized he might also enjoy the opportunity to spend more time with Bella. "Unfortunately, I cannot attend because I'm meeting with a stonemason about a crumbling outer wall."

"Well, we will be glad to take Michael. He would be no trouble," Grandmère said.

William turned to Michael. "Do you promise to behave?"

"I do, I pwomise."

"Arf!" Lacey barked approval.

"Very well. Since Lacey's given her approval, the matter is settled, Michael. You shall accompany the ladies to town and uncover more about this buried treasure."

Michael whooped with delight, his excitement bubbling over in an uncontainable burst of energy.

"What's this about buried treasure?" a tall, dark-haired man asked as he strode into the room, a curious glint sparking in his eye. A hint of gray at his temples lent an air of distinction to his otherwise youthful features. His gaze landed on the dowager countess, and his tone shifted to one of polite stiffness. "Mother. My apologies for the intrusion—I wasn't aware we had guests for tea."

"Uncle Stephen, we have visitors," Bella exclaimed, rising from her seat with a touch of nervous energy. A faint strain in her voice caught William's attention, though she masked it with a smile. "This is our neighbor, Viscount William Dudley, and his younger brother, Master Michael Dudley," she continued, her tone a trifle stiff. "Lord Dudley, may I present my uncle, the Earl of Bridgewater." She turned back to the older man. "Uncle, would you care to join us?"

The earl surveyed the room with an aloof air, his smile clearly forced. "Ah. I've heard of you, Dudley. A hero, I believe? Thought it seems fate has deprived us of a proper introduction—until now," he said, his voice clipped.

"Yes, we have just taken up residence," William said as he

rose, extending his hand to the earl. "My sincerest condolences on the loss of your brother, Lord Miles Bridgewater. As I understand it, it was a very unfortunate accident that took his life."

As William spoke, he couldn't help but notice the tension radiating from the earl—a simmering unease just beneath the surface. The earl's gaze flicked sharply, first toward his mother, then toward Bella, carrying a shadow of barely restrained anger.

Despite the undercurrent of hostility, he accepted William's hand and nodded curtly. "And what of this so-called buried treasure?" he asked in a surly tone, his skepticism evident.

"Oh, Grandmère mentioned a fabled story about a treasure in the area," Bella replied quickly, her tone calm. "Michael is simply fascinated by anything to do with pirates—that's all."

"So, it's nothing more than an old wives' tale," Bridgewater said dismissively, his irritation cutting sharply in Bella's direction.

"Not an old wives' tale," his mother interjected firmly. "We are going into the village tomorrow to make some inquiries."

The earl let out an impatient huff. "Well, when you're done with your *inquiries*," he replied, his tone laced with sarcasm, "perhaps you should take your granddaughter to the modiste's shop while you're in town and see that she's fitted for a proper ball gown."

"And why would Bella need a new ball gown?" Lady Bridgewater said, with narrowed eyes.

"We've just received an invitation. Baron Darkmoor is hosting a ball in two weeks, and we shall all be attending," the earl announced, his tone curt. Turning to his mother, he added, "Mother, dear, please ensure Bella has a proper gown for the occasion. Baron Darkmoor is a significant figure in the area, and it would be prudent to cultivate his goodwill."

His gaze flicked pointedly toward William before he continued. "Regrettably, I won't be able to join your little tea party, Bella. I have pressing estate matters to attend to," he said, his tone cool and devoid of the familial warmth one might expect from an uncle. With that, the earl strode from the room, leaving a tangible tension behind.

William couldn't help but notice the matching expressions etched on the grandmothers' faces and the flicker of unease in Bella's lovely eyes. He had yet to make Baron Darkmoor's acquaintance, but he resolved to learn everything he could about the man and why the earl seemed determined to court his favor.

CHAPTER FIVE

STEPHEN STORMED FROM the drawing room, his emotions swirling like a tempest. He glanced back at the scene behind him. Bella laughed at something cute the little boy had said. Grandmother Harrington was laughing and fawning over both guests. Even his mother—who was normally reserved—was animated and enjoying a cheery conversation with Viscount Dudley and the young boy. The stark contrast of their merriment to his own inner darkness only deepened the churning in his gut.

It felt like they were living in two different worlds—he lived in one plagued by burdens only he understood. He had squandered another small fortune on the baron, a man known for his ability to read a room and predict his opponents' weaknesses, a man of extreme wealth and a mysterious past. Word in London was that the baron's fortune rivaled that of the richest peers.

The only reason Stephen had gambled today was to win back some of his losses. But his strategy once again had come up short. He couldn't recall ever succeeding against the baron—except, perhaps, at a few very early hands. That was years ago. Every time Stephen tried to win, he just fell deeper into debt. At first, he had hoped to reverse his luck to prove to Miles that he was worthy as a man, something he'd never felt when compared to his honorable brother.

Since his brother's death, Stephen had hoped his mother

would have turned to him for advice on financial matters. Which would have given him access to her considerable fortune. But no—she trusted the family solicitors, the sons of the old codgers his late father and brother had always relied upon. And that left Stephen with little more than a title and mounting frustration.

If only he had pursued his painting, as his brother had encouraged him to do for years. When he returned from the Napoleonic Wars, having seen things no one would want to see, he should have taken time to do something that would help soothe his spirit. Painting could have helped. Had he taken his brother's advice, he might have achieved success by now—enough to secure the financial independence he so desperately craved. But instead, he had succumbed to the irresistible vices that had shadowed his life: wine, women, and gaming. Or more precisely in his case, cards.

This time, he had even tried to avoid the temptation of the free-flowing liquor—a lavish indulgence generously provided by the baron. All the food and drink one could desire, and then some. A fleeting thought crossed his mind—perhaps the baron had plotted against him. But he quickly dismissed the idea. He'd never accuse the baron of such a scheme. Stephen was many things, but a coward he was not, and blaming others for his troubles would be beneath him.

Regret coursed through him as he recalled the last words he'd exchanged with his brother—shortly before Miles's untimely death. They'd had a heated argument over his gambling losses and excessive drinking.

Even then it had been too late to stop. His debts had already mounted to such an extent that the only solution was to keep playing and hope to win. Alas, his losses had been the only consistent thing in his life. The baron would be arriving soon, and the only thing he had told Stephen was that his debt had risen to a level that he now needed further concessions to cover his bills. Stephen could feel the weight of the baron's demands on his shoulders. He needed a plan… and he needed it now.

A tap at the study door sounded, and Garrett stepped inside. "My lord, Baron Darkmoor has arrived. Shall I show him in?"

Damn! He needed a few more minutes to think. Unfortunately, he had nowhere to put Darkmoor. He couldn't leave him waiting in the drawing room because his mother was entertaining Dudley and the boy. And he certainly wouldn't have Garrett use his mother's parlor. She was very strict about the use of that room. His brother had always let her have her way. And now wasn't the time to get into a row with his mother over who was in charge.

Swallowing, he said, "Show him in, Garrett."

A few moments later, the baron strode in. Garrett bowed and closed the door behind them.

"May I offer you some brandy, baron?"

"I appreciate the offer, Bridgewater, but I'll get right to the point," the baron said, seating himself in the cordovan leather chair across from Stephen's desk. "Your debt has gotten to the point that I must demand a larger payment on it. Or call in the entire amount."

"I… I see," Stephen said, hating the tremble in his voice that betrayed his anxiousness. He had anticipated this, but still, hearing it out loud caused his insides to quake. If Darkmoor called in the debt, how in the blazes would he cover it? He didn't have two farthings to rub together. Stephen cleared his throat. "I must speak to my man of business. It may take a few days." Hopefully, that might buy him some time.

"I would advise you not to wait," the baron said in a smoothly sinister tone. Reaching out, he picked up a small miniature of Bella sitting on the corner of Stephen's desk.

Stephen had planned to remove his brother's personal effects from the desk but had forgotten.

"Your niece?" the man asked.

"Yes. That's Bella," Stephen said with a gulp. The man had a strange glint in his eye.

"She is already out in Society, no?" Darkmoor queried.

"Yes… but she has been in mourning for her father," Stephen said.

"Ah! Her father. I knew the former Lord Bridgewater. Never set foot in my establishment. A very responsible and respectable gentleman. He would have generously provided for his daughter. Perhaps her fortune could be your gain."

Stephen didn't miss the insult and was appalled at the direction the conversation was taking. He could not steal from his niece, not even to save his own skin… could he?

"He did, and even though I am her guardian, I do not have access to the funds her father set aside for her." He hoped that would end the conversation.

"Then you might have to sell an unentailed property. May I suggest you come up with a solution to your dilemma, as I will be calling your debts due in two weeks," Darkmoor said.

"But you can't. I… I mean, surely there is an amount we can agree on in the interim," Stephen said, frustrated at the way this man made him feel. "And my niece owns…" He realized what he was saying and closed his mouth, suddenly angry that his father and brother had left him out of their business dealings. He was the second son and should have been included in the various duties and holdings of the estate. While his late brother had left everything secure, it was under the helm of the blasted solicitors.

"Ah. Perhaps we are onto something. I assume your niece owns this property."

Stephen was surprised that Darkmoor had guessed correctly, but nodded, thinking if he opened his mouth to speak, he would dig a deeper hole.

"And she comes of age… when?" Darkmoor demanded.

"When she turns twenty-one, according to my brother's will," Stephen said, suddenly realizing where this might be going.

"I've had the pleasure of seeing your niece in the village. A rare beauty. And quite spirited, from what I have observed." Darkmoor smiled broadly. "A man would be lucky to have such a splendid young woman as a wife."

A chill went up Stephen's spine. He knew full well what the baron meant.

"I would like to marry her. I will court her, and we shall become betrothed. My ball is perfect for the beginning of our... relationship."

"No... that won't do. She intends to marry for love," Stephen said. When he saw the scowl on the baron's face, he wished he hadn't.

"No, it *will* do. I will woo her first, of course. But once we are married, perhaps I will forgive some of your debt—depending on the value of her dowry," Darkmoor said.

"The house is not part of her dowry," Stephen blurted.

"Ah... but when she weds, whatever she owns becomes the property of her husband."

Stephen had seen the paperwork. It specified that the house would belong to Bella, whether she married or not. But he held his tongue. "Only if my niece agrees," he said. He couldn't bring himself to force her against her will, if there was anything he could do about it. What a mess. Now he was dragging everyone he loved into the same hole he had dug for himself.

"Then I must make sure she falls under my spell." Darkmoor smiled that predatory smile once more as he got up from the chair. "I will hold off on demanding full payment. We will work on the betrothal, instead. Do we have an agreement?" The baron held out his hand and, shocking himself to his core, Stephen gripped it.

The next morning
The town of Dover

THE BLACK LACQUER Bridgewater carriage pulled up in front of the Sweet Shop, and a small group disembarked. Bella was excited and a tad nervous. She had never met a gypsy before. She looked down at the adorable boy who had insisted on being her escort. Master Michael Dudley had been a delightful companion as they drove into town from the manor house—and was full of questions.

"Do you think the lady will be here, Gwand-mare?"

"Honey, I think so," Lady Harrington said, giving a gentle pat to his golden curls. "She rents a room at the back of Abernathy's Tea Shop. That is where she tells her fortunes. I thought she might come here for her midday meal. This is where I encountered her last. Let me ask the proprietor. If she's not here, he may know where to find her. We are glad you and your brother joined us today."

As the small group entered the apothecary, Bella's mouth watered from the aromas of chocolate, citrus, almond, and cinnamon swirling in the air.

"And she will tell us about the pirates?" Michael asked.

"She may know a lot about pirates in the area," Bella said, in awe of her grandmothers, both enjoying showing this little boy a good time.

"I feel certain she will," Lady Bridgewater said, nodding to a woman sitting in the back, enjoying a pot of tea. "Elise, doesn't that look like the Roma gypsy in the corner?"

"Arf!" Lacey barked as if to remind them of her presence.

"Good dog," Michael said. "I promised her a biscuit. I should probably give her a biscuit before I eat one."

"And she listened to you? You met her only yesterday," Lady Bridgewater said, with a hint of surprise. "And giving a biscuit to her before you eat one is very generous. You can have mine— once we are seated and have ordered. I had one with my tea for breakfast."

"Thank you!" the little boy said, looking around the room. "I'm very excited. Aren't you, Lacey?"

The dog thumped her tail excitedly on the wooden floor.

"If you will excuse me, we would like to speak to the lady in the back," Lady Harrington said. "Bella, we will be right back."

Bella nodded as her grandmothers stepped away to speak with the Roma gypsy. Bella was curious about the woman, but didn't want to crowd the fortune teller, especially with a boy and dog in tow. Her grandmothers were all smiles when they returned a few minutes later.

"Madame Vorest will talk to us," Grandmère said, leading the way. "She is most gracious. "And she is most keen on sharing the story about the pirate's treasure."

"I can't wait," Michael said, excitedly rubbing his little hands.

"What a lovely boy and young lady," the gypsy cooed as she waved them over to her table. "Come here, my dear girl, and sit by me."

The server rushed to add more chairs around the table and take their orders.

"You are most kind to indulge us," Lady Harrington said. "This is Michael, a dear friend of our family."

"I want to hear about the pirates, if you please," he said, puffing out his chest.

"Ah… the pirate tale. I will be glad to speak of it." Madame Vorest looked at Michael. "The story is certain to capture your imagination. But first, who is this beautiful young woman?" she asked, grabbing Bella's hand.

"This is our granddaughter, Lady Bella Connolly," Lady Harrington said.

Bella's lips curved up into a polite smile. "I'm glad to meet you, Madame Vorest." The old woman intrigued Bella, and yet there was something about the fortune teller that made her nervous as well. Madame Vorest had expressive brown eyes and dark, wavy hair threaded with silver that cascaded about her shoulders. A bright scarf covered the top of her head, keeping her hair in place. She wore layers of vibrant, patterned skirts—red, gold, and emerald—that complemented her earrings and bangle bracelets. Bella was fascinated by the freedom that her clothing gave her—a big improvement, she thought, over the underclothing that *she* had to wear.

"So, young man, you are interested in pirates," Madame Vorest said, gently taking Michael's small hand in hers. She turned it over and looked at it. "This line tells me you have a strong spirit of adventure. I can see why you want to know about pirates."

"One day, I want to have my own ship and sail the seas!" he exclaimed.

"All the seas?"

"Yes… and sail all over the world."

"Well, certainly the treasure would help with that," the gypsy said, smiling.

"It will be my first treasure. But I will work hard and find more," he said. "I'll have to find myself a deep, dark cave somewhere, so I can use it to hide all the treasure chests I'll discover on my journeys."

"Of course," Madame Vorest said, nodding in agreement. "Young man, this is a very old tale, maybe two hundred years old. There is a place in Dover near the sea with a buried treasure— treasure that has been buried for more than two hundred years. Many have searched for this treasure, but no one has found it. It is said that the treasure is in a wooden chest, lined with velvet and filled with jewels."

"What kind of jewels?" Michael asked in a voice filled with awe.

"Oh, perhaps diamonds and rubies… emeralds, too," she added.

"What was the pirate's name?" Michael asked, his eyes shining with curiosity as he leaned forward.

"I don't recall, my little lord," the gypsy replied with a mysterious smile, her voice low and melodic. Her dark eyes glittered with mischief as she added, "But names are not what make a story memorable. Now, would you like to hear the tale?"

"Yes, please," Michael said with a firm nod. "If I don't know the story well, then I won't be able to find the treasure."

"Hmm… That is very astute, Master Michael," the dowager

countess said with a knowing wink, her tone teasing but affectionate.

"Please, begin with your tale," Lady Harrington encouraged her with a warm smile.

The old woman inclined her head, her bangle bracelets and earrings catching the light as she began. "There once was a pirate and a prince," she said, her voice weaving the words with the cadence of a spell.

Bella watched as Michael leaned forward, completely captivated, his small hands gripping the edge of his chair. She even found herself drawn in, despite the faint prickle of unease at the back of her mind.

"The pirate," the old woman continued, "was bold and daring, with charm enough to steal more than gold. He vowed to win the hand of a beautiful young maiden, offering her a chest of jewels—treasures plundered from far-off lands. But the prince"—she paused, her tone softening—"had no such riches. He offered her only his heart—pure and true. Now, tell me, *mon petit*, who do you think she chose?"

Michael scrunched up his face, his nose wrinkling as he considered the question. With dramatic flair, he declared, "The pirate!" Then his face twisted into an overly exaggerated "blech" that sent Bella and the older women into a fit of laughter.

The gypsy woman chuckled, her bangles jingling as she reached out to tap Michael on the nose. "Ah, but you see, the pirate was lost at sea in a terrible storm on his way to retrieve his treasure. The maiden, clever as she was, saw the truth behind his glittering promise and chose the prince's heart instead. They married and lived happily ever after."

Michael groaned, crossing his arms with a pout. "Blech," he said again, clearly unimpressed. "I would've picked the pirate. Sailing the world on a ship sounds much more fun than being stuck in some boring castle with a prince."

The women laughed again, but Bella's thoughts wandered. There was something about the gypsy's story—something that prickled at the edges of her memory. She'd heard rumors before, whispered tales of a smuggler's treasure hidden somewhere near the cliffs. It was said there were tunnels beneath the ground, carved long ago by men who risked their lives for illicit trade.

As the laughter subsided, the old woman's gaze shifted. Her dark, knowing eyes met Bella's, and for a moment, the room seemed to still. A shiver ran through Bella, as if the gypsy's gaze had peeled back the layers of the story, revealing a deeper truth meant only for her.

She swallowed hard and looked away, but the feeling lingered. The pirate in the story may have been lost at sea, but she couldn't shake the thought that another, far more dangerous pirate might truly exist.

"I wonder where it could be," Michael whispered.

"No one has been fortunate enough to uncover it," the gypsy replied, lowering her voice to a conspiratorial hush. The room seemed to draw closer around her as she spoke. "Countless souls have been drawn to the promise of unimaginable riches. They say the treasure lies on a property that hugs the shoreline, buried deep within a hidden tunnel that leads to the sea. Many brave men have risked everything to find it, but all have returned empty-handed—if they returned at all."

As Bella listened intently, the gypsy's words conjured vivid images of daring pirates and hidden passageways, and her thoughts began to wander again. She found herself thinking back to the other day, to her first encounter with Viscount William Dudley. It was a day painted in the sharp hues of memory—so vivid she could almost feel the sea breeze on her face again.

She had thought herself unlucky at first, nearly tumbling down the rocky cliff toward the ocean after getting her foot caught in soft soil and twigs. But the viscount had appeared seemingly out of nowhere, catching her before she fell. His golden hair had caught the sunlight, and his sky-blue eyes held both concern and a charm she hadn't expected. She'd thanked him, flustered, only to catch the flicker of a smile that had lingered in her mind ever since.

Her gaze shifted to Michael, whose rapt attention was fixed on the gypsy. *Caves,* Bella thought suddenly. Were there caves on her father's—no, her uncle's—land? The idea sent a ripple of curiosity through her. She knew the cliffs were riddled with rocky crags and crevices, but could one of them lead to the legendary tunnel? And if so, what secrets might it hold?

She shook herself slightly, returning her attention to the gypsy's story, though the thought lingered. Perhaps the treasure wasn't the only mystery waiting to be uncovered along the shoreline.

Could she have stepped through the roof of one of those caves that day? Looking back, she recalled that the ground had been loose and didn't feel as solid beneath her feet. She also remembered that she had stepped into something, causing her to lose her balance. She'd have to be careful in the future.

"That is all I know of the tale of the pirate's treasure, young man," the gypsy concluded, her words lingering in the air like a whispered secret. Then her dark gaze shifted to Bella, and her expression softened. "My dear, I could not help but notice the worry in your eyes."

With a graceful movement, the Roma gypsy reached across the table, her fingers warm against Bella's skin as she took her hand. Her touch was delicate yet grounding, and as she gently turned Bella's palm upward, she began to trace the faint lines etched there. Her fingers glided over Bella's lifeline with an almost reverent precision.

"I can sense that you are destined for great love in the future," the gypsy murmured, her melodic voice carrying a mysterious weight. But then her expression darkened, a shadow passing over her features. "However," she added in a lower tone, "there will also be great danger..."

Bella froze, her breath catching in her throat. Startled, she pulled her hand back as if burned, a chill racing down her spine at the gypsy's forbidding words.

"You are scaring my granddaughter. Why?" Grandmère demanded, her voice sharp with anger and protectiveness.

The gypsy lowered her gaze, her demeanor suddenly contrite. "I am sorry, my lady," she said softly. "But her fortune needed to be told. She must know what it contains—for her own sake."

Bella's heart hammered in her chest as she stared at the gypsy, torn between disbelief and unease. The room seemed to grow quieter, the air heavier, as if the weight of the woman's words had cast a shadow over them all.

"But you didn't ask her…" blustered her grandmother, frustrated. "I asked if you would talk about the pirate treasure, not danger and great love."

"Wh-why or h-how would I be in danger?" Bella asked, her voice sounding wobbly, even to herself.

"I do not know the details and cannot say, although I am sorry that I frightened you, my dear. But please do take care and be aware. When you find that great love, you will know. In here." The fortune teller put a balled fist to her chest.

"I… thank you, Madame Vorest," Bella said. But she didn't feel grateful. Having danger in her future was the last thing she'd expected to hear—and the last thing she wanted.

CHAPTER SIX

Two days later
Bridgewater Stables

"IT'S BEEN A few days, sweet Winterborne. I'll bet you thought I'd forgotten you," Bella said softly, holding out a carrot for her late father's horse. "I've missed you."

The black thoroughbred with a mark resembling a white snowflake on its forehead accepted the carrot with a gentle nuzzle, then neighed softly.

Bella stepped onto the bottom slat of the gate, leaning over to press a kiss to the horse's forehead. The familiar scent of leather and hay mixed with the comforting presence of Winterborne brought an ache to her chest. Being near him was like holding a piece of her father close—soothing yet tinged with sorrow. She suspected the horse felt the same. The groom had assured her that Winterborne was eating and obedient during his morning exercises, but the grief in his eyes mirrored her own.

Bella sighed, brushing her fingers lightly over the soft patch of white fur. "I know how you feel, my friend. We'll muddle through this sadness together, won't we? Do you want another carrot?"

The large horse whinnied and bobbed his head as if in reply, dark eyes sparking briefly with life.

"Ha! I thought so. I brought a pocket full just for you." She reached into her pelisse, pulled out several more carrots, and held one up teasingly.

"I thought we might find you here, Bella," came a warm, familiar voice from behind.

She turned, her heart quickening as she met William's gaze. Those sparkling sapphire-blue eyes never failed to captivate her, their intensity both unsettling and exhilarating. His easy smile sent a pleasant warmth spiraling through her. Why was it that whenever he was near, her composure seemed to slip? She forced herself to focus, hoping the brisk morning air might disguise the color rising to her cheeks.

"William. Michael. How nice to see you both. Good morning," she greeted them. "I was just talking to Winterborne. And feeding him these." She held out a carrot. "He's much more chipper since he's gained access to his favorite treat."

Michael stepped forward, his small hands gripping the gate as he peered up at the horse. "He looks sad," he said.

Bella looked again at the horse—this time, looking into his eyes—and noted that despite the carrot treats, the creature did appear sad. "You're very observant, Michael. Winterborne does look sad." She paused, stroking the horse's nose gently. "He was my father's. They were very close, and Winterborne misses him."

Michael's big, curious eyes fixed on her. "What happened to your father?" he asked softly.

Bella drew in a steadying breath, the weight of the memory pressing on her. "He passed away from injuries after being thrown from Winterborne," she explained. "Father loved riding in the mornings to see the sunrise, but that day… something must have spooked Winterborne. It was foggy, and when Father fell, he hit his head on a rock." Her voice faltered for a moment, but she forced a small, reassuring smile. "He never recovered."

Michael was quiet for a moment, then tilted his head. "Do you blame him?" he asked, his youthful sincerity cutting straight to her heart.

The question made her pause. She crouched slightly, meeting the boy's earnest gaze. "That's a fair question, Michael. But no, I don't blame Winterborne. He loved my father very much and would never have wanted to hurt him. We don't know what frightened him that day, but I'm sure he wishes things had been different too."

Michael nodded solemnly, his missing front teeth making his lips curl as he thought. "Then why don't you *wide* him?"

"Michael, you go too far," William gently admonished his brother. "I'm sorry…"

Bella held up her hand to stop William's apology. "Why did you ask me that, Michael?" she asked gently.

The boy fidgeted with something in his pockets. "I don't know why," he finally said. "I just thought of it."

"My mother wrote me, shortly before she passed, and said that Michael seemed to prefer the animals to playing with children in the area," William said. "He told her that the children could be mean, but animals were never mean to him. Perhaps that was the beginning of his connection with animals. My father's horses fascinated him. Unfortunately, Father died while my mother was pregnant with Michael, and he missed out on knowing his father's gentle soul."

"And your mother?" Bella asked softly.

A shadow crossed William's face as he replied. "She died of scarlet fever almost three years ago—they had an outbreak near our home. After she passed, Michael was ferried between relatives in my absence—so, as soon as it was feasible, I made changes so my brother could live with me." He playfully tousled Michael's curly hair. "There's no sense in having wealth if you can't use it to help those you cherish."

"I agree," Bella said, absorbing his words. She knelt to be at eye level with Michael. "So, you think Winterborne is… lonely?" she asked.

"He is," Michael said with unmistakable assurance. "I see it in his eyes. His heart hurts, my lady. Maybe he wants you to *wide* him."

Bella stood and turned to look at her father's magnificent

thoroughbred, focusing intently on his large, soulful eyes. She could have sworn she saw a glimmer of moisture—perhaps a tear—glistening there. "I think you're right," she murmured. What a sensitive boy to understand Winterborne's distress. "Do you know how to ride, Michael?" she asked.

"No, my lady," he said, shaking his head and looking longingly up at Winterborne.

Her eyes met William's as he cleared his throat. "I haven't had the time to teach him yet," he said.

Michael straightened his shoulders. "It's all wight, Will. You're busy with all your *busy-ness*."

William exchanged a smile with Bella.

"Thank you for your understanding, Michael, but I hope to remedy the situation soon," he said, patting his brother on the shoulder.

Michael nodded, beaming. He turned to gaze up at the horse, perhaps igniting a shared dream between the two of them. "Maybe one day I'll even ride Winterborne."

The pounding of horse's hooves approached, and a rider swiftly dismounted. "My lord, an urgent message arrived at the manor house for you," the rider said, pulling a sealed missive from his saddlebag.

"Thank you, Franklin," William said, accepting the document and breaking the seal. After taking a moment to peruse it, he looked at Bella and Michael. "Michael, we need to get back to the house, immediately."

The boy nodded. Then he turned and waved at the horse. "Winterborne, I will see you tomorrow." The horse lowered his head, and Michael gave his nose a gentle pat.

"If it's all right with you, William, I would be happy to bring Michael home in a couple of hours," Bella said. "I thought he might like to meet Flo, the barn cat. She's almost ready to have kittens, and we are trying to get her comfortable. Michael might have a few good ideas for us." She smiled.

Michael turned to his brother, his eyes hopeful. "I'd very

much like to see Flo if you will permit it."

"Are you certain you don't mind bringing him home?" William asked Bella.

"I would be happy to. I'll return him in a couple of hours."

William knelt and gently squeezed his brother's shoulder. "I want you to mind Bella, and don't go wandering off anywhere." He turned to her. "He loves animals, and they seem to respond favorably." Looking down at Michael, he said again, "Listen to Lady Bella, Michael."

"I pwomise, William," the little boy said.

"Thank you, Bella," William said with a smile.

Bella felt another rush of heat rising to her cheeks. *Lord, I need to stop blushing every time he's near.* She tucked a loose strand of hair behind her ear, hoping he hadn't noticed.

Although she'd only met them a few days ago, she adored Michael's sweet innocence and the way his curiosity lit up the world around him. And as for William... Well, he had a way of looking at her that made her pulse quicken and her thoughts scatter. But surely that was nothing more than... what, admiration? A bit of harmless infatuation?

She shook the thought away. Yet as she glanced in the direction that William had gone, a wistful thought tugged at her heart.

I wish I could have had more time with him.

WILLIAM RACED ACROSS the sprawling grounds, the manor house looming larger with each pounding step. His heart thundered in sync with the urgency of the message Franklin had handed him— a mystery demanding swift unraveling.

Time was critical. The bright afternoon sunlight pouring through the high windows of the manor would soon begin its descent, and its glow was essential for illuminating the fine details of his tools and the subtle patterns hidden within the cryptic message.

Bursting through the front door, he strode directly to his study. Unlocking the cabinet with practiced efficiency, he retrieved his cipher tools and laid them out on the great oak desk. The cipher wheel, a marvel of interlocking discs, glinted faintly in the sunlight, its precise mechanisms promising to reveal the message's secrets. Beside it lay his cipher grid, meticulously crafted to uncover order in chaos, and his well-worn codebook, its pages filled with substitutions, encryptions, and his annotations—hours of study bound in ink and paper.

Deciphering messages for the Crown wasn't just a duty, it was a fascinating hunt for the truth. Each encrypted note was a battle of wits, a silent contest between himself and the unseen adversaries weaving their schemes in the shadows. Smugglers, spies, traitors—they all left trails in their intricate webs of deceit, and it was his task to dismantle them, one thread at a time.

Within the encoded message lay the answers—a plan to thwart, a danger to prevent—and the clock was ticking. Unfortunately, the missive's arrival had been ill-timed, pulling William away from Bella. He had gone to the stables not just to see her— though he couldn't deny how much he enjoyed her company— but also to uncover more about her uncle. Something about the man's demise gnawed at him, a quiet but persistent unease.

When he'd met Bella's uncle three days prior, the man had struck him as deeply morose, as though weighed down by some inner turmoil. Yet his mood had shifted abruptly, his melancholy giving way to an unsettling anger when he found Bella and the other women laughing and enjoying themselves. That reaction had been both curious and disturbing. What could inspire such bitterness, especially directed at his niece?

William couldn't shake the feeling that there was more to the man's hostility than mere disapproval of frivolity. And while his instincts urged him to tread carefully, his growing fondness for Bella—and his sense of duty to protect her—made it impossible to ignore.

A knock sounded at the door, followed by Harlow stepping into the study. "My lord," he said, carrying a tray. "Anticipating the importance of the missive, I asked the cook to prepare a tray of sandwiches, cheese, and fruit for you."

"Mrs. Bradberry did a wonderful job," William said with a grateful smile. "As usual, you have anticipated my needs perfectly, Harlow." He often became absorbed in the intricate patterns of ciphers, losing all sense of time—often even forgetting to eat—as he delved deeper into his work. "Thank you," he said. "By the way, Michael should be returning in a few hours. Lady Bella will be accompanying him." A hint of anticipation laced his words. He hoped he might see her again if he was finished with his work.

"I will be attuned to their arrival," Harlow said. "Let me know if there's anything else you require, my lord," he added with a respectful nod, exiting the room.

Hours passed, marked only by the dimming light outside. At last, William had deciphered the note before him. As the final letters fell into place, an icy shiver coursed through him.

Pied Piper is near.

Remain vigilant.

The losses mount, and more will follow.

Beware the path ahead—

Danger waits in the shadows.

He takes what cannot be replaced.

The young. The innocent. They vanish into the night, their cries swallowed by the tide.

Once taken, they are never seen again.

The Piper plays his tune, and those who follow do not return.

The path to his warren is well hidden, his network vast.

Whispers of his trade spread through the docks, but fear silences those who know too much.

Watch. Wait. Be wary of those in power around you.
He moves among them, masked by wealth and influence.
His deception is his greatest weapon.

He is closer than you think…

William rubbed his bleary eyes and stretched. It had been an intensive decoding. His thoughts turned to his brother, and he reached for the bellpull. A few moments later, Harlow stepped inside, ready to assist.

"Yes, my lord?"

"Harlow, has my brother returned?" William asked.

"Yes, sir. Lady Bella and Lady Harrington dropped him off a few hours ago," the butler said. "I believe his new governess, Mrs. Randal, tucked him into bed."

Relief washed over William, but an underlying tension remained. He reread the missive he'd just finished decoding, and a chill ran down his spine. *The Pied Piper is near.*

It was no longer just an ominous warning—it was a confirmation. The Piper was here, in Dover, operating in the very area William called home. Where Michael lived. Where other innocent children lived, unaware of the shadow lurking among them.

His grip on the paper tightened.

He had left active duty behind. He had resigned himself to a quieter life, tending to his responsibilities as a viscount and raising his younger brother. But duty, it seemed, was not done with him.

He could not turn away—not now.

The Pied Piper preyed upon the vulnerable, stealing children in the dead of night, his web stretching beyond the docks and alleyways, reaching into the highest echelons of society.

And he was close.

William exhaled slowly, his pulse steadying. He would remain vigilant. He would not allow another child to be taken—not while he still had the power to stop it.

Sitting back in his leather chair, he closed his eyes and reflected on what he knew about the area. The face that repeatedly came to his mind was that of Bella's uncle. Despite his having deciphered the note, he found himself fixated on Lord Stephen Bridgewater.

Something felt off about the man, and William was determined to investigate. Bridgewater's behavior troubled him, though he couldn't be sure if his concern stemmed from his preoccupation with Lady Bella. *But was it just a preoccupation?* He suspected the man was harboring a secret, and William wanted to know what it was.

Reaching into his desk drawer, he retrieved a key from a recessed area in the bottom. He took it upstairs to his room, opened a box, and withdrew a costume he hadn't donned in over a year. He would disguise himself and follow the earl.

Something is amiss with this man, and I will find out what it is.

CHAPTER SEVEN

Cliffton Abbey

"**P**ATRICK, I WILL require your assistance putting on my disguise," William said.

"I haven't seen that wig since France," his valet said, retrieving a cotton cap from the drawer.

Patrick had been William's batman during his time in the military. William appreciated Patrick's skills with theatrical makeup—he had secured a theater job he held for a short time after his release from the military. "Light on the makeup. All right?" he said, fidgeting as Patrick pulled out his kit.

"Ye don't want to be recognized, do ye?" Patrick said, applying some cream. He withdrew the wax they had fashioned into a scar and adhered it to William's forehead just above his brow. "If we allow a fringe of hair to hang over the scar, it'll give ye a bit of a rogue effect. The scar will help."

William groaned. "I was thinking a mustache and pair of glasses would work fine."

"It's a small scar," Patrick said, withdrawing a pair of spectacles and ignoring William's irritation. "Don't worry. These spectacles have no prescription, my lord. I picked up several new pairs from a shop near one of the theaters in London that are different from the pairs you've worn in the past."

William nodded. "Thank you. I hadn't expected the need to wear another disguise, given that I am no longer on active duty, but there's a man I need to follow. He's already met me as Lord Dudley. I need to make sure he doesn't recognize me."

"I'll make sure of that, sir. I have one more thing to do… and I'm done." Patrick held up a looking glass to William's face.

William regarded his reflection, tugging a little on the wig over his ears. "I always forget how itchy it is."

"Yes. The wig is horsehair. I should have gotten a better one for you, but unfortunately, the shop I visited didn't have any alternatives," Patrick said. "I'm sorry, my lord. I'll correct that problem as soon as I can, so if ye require a disguise in the future, ye will have a wig that will not cause itchiness."

"I don't recognize myself," William said. "You've done well, Patrick, thank you. It's dark, so I'll take my leave through the secret exit you discovered when we first arrived. It's hard to believe there are so many secret passages. I spoke with Franklin earlier and he should have brought the small carriage around by now. The unmarked black one."

"Ye think the earl will lead you to what ye're looking for tonight?" Patrick asked.

Not expecting the question, William paused and thought about it. "I'm not sure what I'll find, but I can't shake the feeling that I need to do this. The man was acting extremely strange. I don't know the what or the why, but I feel it's important."

"This part of England has periodically been ripe with pirates and smuggling," Patrick said. "The house has been here for a while, and many were probably built out of the needs of the occupants. The secret passage that leaves from yer rooms hasn't been used in years, based on the vermin and spiders I found in there."

"Damn convenient to have that passageway. I appreciate your foresight in making sure no other servants became aware of it," William said.

"Think nothing of it. Besides, Harlow took care of that for me. The man's great with the staff. From what I saw, a labyrinth of tunnels exists below the manor; I'll be happy to help ye explore them when the time is right."

William appreciated Patrick's skills and forthrightness. The man had been with him throughout his years in France, and he trusted him completely. "You know I'll do better if I don't concentrate on the spiders," he said, chuckling.

"I think they'll be trying to avoid you, my lord," Patrick returned, equally mirthful.

"One can hope," William said with an arched brow. "I should be going." He stood. "Thank goodness Michael fell asleep quickly. But he's gotten a taste of the stables, and we both know how much he likes animals. It would not be unheard of for him to slip out to the stables. Please remind Mrs. Randal to keep an eye on him—remind her he's been known to walk in his sleep. I plan to spend more time with him, teaching him to ride and fish, things his father might have done."

"Certainly. I'll take care of it. You be careful," Patrick said, as William strode to the bookcase in his room.

He took a deep breath. "I'm off—this time, I promise." He reached for a worn, leather-bound edition of Shakespeare's complete plays, triggering a secret hinge that smoothly opened the bookcase to reveal a narrow passageway. He lit a lamp and stepped out, closing the bookcase behind him.

DRESSED IN DARK clothing, William easily hid in the shadowy confines of his carriage, a short distance from the Bridgewater house. By nightfall, a thick fog had rolled over the area, making it unnecessary for Franklin to extinguish the carriage lanterns while they waited to see if the earl would leave.

Everything was going well except for the damn wig. He wondered if the itchy feeling was due to more than just the horsehair, but decided not to dwell on that. He'd ask Patrick to add a human-hair beard to the list, as well as the wig. The only things that didn't itch were the wire-rimmed spectacles.

Within thirty minutes, a black coach exited the Bridgewater estate, turning right and heading into the town of Dover. William knew little about the gaming rooms in Dover but felt confident he could shadow the activities of the Earl of Bridgewater.

About twenty minutes later, the Bridgewater coach stopped in front of the Winking Mariner, a tavern well known for the questionable activities that took place within its walls. He watched the earl enter and waited fifteen minutes before leaving his carriage, then instructed Franklin to wait with the other carriages along a side alley.

William squinted against the haze of smoke that clung to the air like a suffocating fog. As his eyes adjusted to the murky gloom, he took in the dreary interior of the tavern. The low ceilings pressed down on the space, their beams blackened with soot from countless tallow candles, which flickered weakly against the oppressive darkness.

Single sconces hung unevenly on the dark-paneled walls, their feeble flames casting a faint, flickering light that seemed to deepen the shadows rather than dispel them. In the corners, where the light barely reached, dubious figures huddled over tankards, their voices lowered to conspiratorial whispers. The smell of stale ale, damp wood, and unwashed bodies permeated the room, an odor that clung to the nostrils like a bad memory. The floor beneath William's boots was sticky with spilled drinks, crushed straw, and dried mud.

As he reached the bar, he looked around the room, searching for more than just the source of the muffled tension that seemed to emanate from every corner. This wasn't just a place to drink—it was a haven for secrets, where men traded more than coin and risked far more than they could afford to lose.

"There's a table in the back," a buxom blonde barmaid said as she edged past him with practiced ease, carrying a tray with sloshing tankards of ale and glasses of gin through the crowd. Bridgewater wasn't in this room, which meant he was probably already in a game somewhere in the tavern. The centuries-old building appeared to sprawl unevenly, its layout betraying the haphazard nature of rough-hewn additions tacked onto the back over the years. Narrow hallways disappeared into the shadows, suggesting a maze of dim, ramshackle extensions that had been built with little regard for form or function.

"I'll have an ale," William said as he leaned against the bar.

The bartender narrowed his eyes, his gaze sharp and assessing, as he turned to the barrel behind him. With practiced efficiency, he pulled the spigot, filling a dented tankard until the froth threatened to spill over. Then, with a flick of his wrist, he slid it down the scarred bar top, the vessel skimming over the worn wood before coming to a halt with a dull thud. "Ye're new."

William paid for his drink and took a sip. "I am supposed to meet a friend in the game room."

"What games are ye looking to play?" the bartender asked, a hint of suspicion in his tone, as he picked up the coin William had left on the counter.

"I'm not particular," William said with casual nonchalance, withdrawing a pound note from his pocket and handing it to the bartender. He used a practiced, rustier tone—one he often adopted when in disguise. "I'm looking for a game… Something to help me unwind from a long day."

"Upstairs. Take the second door," the man said, nodding at the stairwell in the corner, swiftly tucking the bill in his worn apron pocket.

Picking up his drink, William thanked the man and made his way up. The sprawling room was even drearier than downstairs. In one corner was a spirited game of cribbage—the wall behind them bore the marks of their competition, with chalk tally marks etched in uneven lines. In the center of the room was a table for six with a card game underway. Five men were playing and there was one empty chair. William recognized the earl among the players. From observing the man's body language, it appeared he was losing. The only person that seemed to be pleased was the man seated across from Bridgewater. Behind them, a few bystanders huddled, watching with keen interest.

Raucous laughter and energetic shouts of men placing bets drew William's curiosity. A small group of men had gathered. Their eyes were fixed intently on two men throwing darts. The dartboard, crafted from roughly hewn wood and painted with concentric circles, dominated one wall, its surface marked by the wear of countless games. A young sailor appeared to be winning, and when a new game was announced, the young man ordered drinks for everyone.

"Mind if I join you?" William inquired, sliding into the empty seat at the card table. A few of the men nodded or grunted a welcome.

"Have my seat," the earl said, his tone dismissive. "I'm not interested in continuing."

"Nonsense," the tall, broad-shouldered man seated across from him said. "You've only just arrived. The night is young."

"Don't be leaving us so soon, guvnor," a barmaid crooned, a practiced smile curving her lips as she wove effortlessly through the crowd to Bridgewater's side. She tossed her dark hair with exaggerated ease, brushing off the slaps and pinches from the men, her laughter as hollow as the ale-stained floor beneath her feet. She placed a drink in front of him. "Nothing but the best for you." Her fingers trailed down Bridgewater's arm as she placed a glass in front of him. "As you requested, milord."

"Fine. I'll do one more hand," Bridgewater said, before taking a sip of the cognac and glaring at the man across from him.

"Need a refill?" the barmaid asked William, her voice more casual than it had been with Bridgewater.

"No. I'll have what he's having," William said.

"The cognac is for special—" she started.

"I'll stay for another hand if you share the stock with him," Bridgewater interjected.

The barmaid cast a quick glance at the man seated across

from Bridgewater as if awaiting his approval. At his subtle nod, she turned to fetch the drink.

William observed the exchange with carefully concealed indifference. It was clear—the tall man opposite Bridgewater was the one in control.

His sleek, dark hair gleamed under the dim light, and his eyes were so deep and impenetrable that it was impossible to distinguish pupil from iris. Though he spoke and dressed like a gentleman, his attire—fine yet understated—was not the sort one would wear to a ball or the theater. It was the clothing of a man who moved in refined circles yet operated in the shadows.

But what struck William most wasn't his appearance—it was the air of absolute authority he exuded, the quiet arrogance of a man who held the fates of every gambler in the room at his whim.

"Allow me to introduce myself," William began. "My name is Bernard Pegram," he said, extending his hand to those around him, and listening carefully as each man introduced himself.

"What do you do, Mr. Pegram?" the man to his left asked.

"I'm an accountant for Streamer Ships. I came in on one of the boats that anchored this morning," William said. He knew it would be difficult for anyone here to challenge him. Men rarely knew the owners of the ships that docked.

"Ah. You must be here to investigate a problem," the tall, broad-shouldered man seated across from William said smoothly, leaning back in his chair and crossing his arms.

Hoping to coax the man into revealing more about himself, William feigned agreement. "Yes, I'm afraid you're right. Wish it weren't so." He looked about the room with a carefully calculated unease, as if harboring burdens too heavy to share. With a faint shake of his head, he added, almost to himself, "I've already said too much." The subtle tension in his tone, paired with the faint hint of worry in his expression, planted the idea that he, too, carried secrets—a ploy designed to spark curiosity in the men watching him.

The man grinned broadly and glanced around the table, his demeanor resembling that of a predator, suggesting that he felt in control of the situation around the table—perhaps in the entire tavern. "You've nothing to worry about here. You're among friends. I'm Baron Darkmoor," he said, with an air of confidence. Seemingly aware that everyone was looking at him, he straightened his posture and puffed out his chest.

"I'm pleased to meet you, my lord," William said, recognizing the name. He had heard it two days ago at Bella's—when the earl announced the upcoming ball. The man seemed to revel in being *known*. A similar invitation had arrived at William's the next day. He had already planned to attend because of Bella, but now he was even more determined to go. There was obviously a deeper connection between the baron and the earl that went beyond their being card-playing cronies.

"I'm the Earl of Bridgewater," Bella's uncle said, maintaining a disinterested air.

"We're playing faro, Pegram. Are you in?" Darkmoor asked, already shuffling the deck of cards.

"Yes, my work can be fraught with troublesome days. Perhaps it'll keep my mind off things I'd rather not think of," William said, hoping his act would provide enough deception to have the baron showing more than just his hand. He'd watch for the palming of cards, suspicious the man was cheating.

"Ah! You must have eyes in the back of your head to keep track of everything on a ship," Darkmoor commented meaningfully, still fingering the cards.

"Indeed, you're correct," William said, peeling off a few pound notes to ante up.

"I believe it's my turn to deal," Darkmoor said, quickly getting the assent of the table.

As the baron dealt the cards, William's sharp gaze caught a subtle flicker of movement—a single ace shifted deftly to the top of the deck. He observed Darkmoor palm the ace, nimbly sliding it into his cuff. A minute later, a second ace that had been flashing on the bottom of the shuffled deck joined it. *Interesting,* William mused, filing the observation away for later. For now, he kept his expression neutral, his lips curling ever so slightly, as though he were merely entertained by the game.

Two hours and five hands later, the earl downed his fourth cognac and, wobbly, pushed back from the table. "That's enough for me," he said.

"Come back tomorrow," the barmaid replied, helping him to the door. "I'm sure your luck will change."

Bridgewater hadn't won a single hand all evening. William had claimed one victory, Darkmoor had taken three, and another man had secured the last. At one point, Bridgewater handed over his vowel to Darkmoor—a desperate gesture—but somehow still managed to settle his debts with William and the other player. By William's calculation, the earl had lost a monkey—a substantial five-hundred-pound blow, enough to sting even a man of title and fortune.

Yet what intrigued William most was Darkmoor's persistent focus on Bridgewater. Throughout the evening, it had become clear that Bridgewater was the intended target of the baron's schemes. But why? What tied these two men together beyond their shared status as gentlemen? Darkmoor's moves were too deliberate to be mere chance, and William's mind churned as he searched for a connection—something buried beneath the veneer of civility, hidden among the shadows of the evening's play.

CHAPTER EIGHT

Cliffton Abbey

IT WAS THE wee hours of the morning when Franklin pulled the coach into the drive of Cliffton Abbey. William was grateful to finally be home. After discreetly following the earl's coach home, to make certain he arrived safely, William had watched from a distance, glad to have remembered his spyglass, as two footmen retrieved Bridgewater from his carriage. With practiced skill, they assisted him and escorted him into the manse.

It seemed Harlow had also been waiting up, for the door opened as William walked up the steps.

William felt he needed to respond to the earlier coded missive from the Home Office—if for no other reason than to detail what had been going on at the Winking Mariner. He had heard about men being fleeced of their life savings in Dover and thought if tonight was any indication, one man stood out as the possible mastermind of that. It was clear that Darkmoor held a substantial influence in town. William would have to figure out what he was using for leverage.

Exhaling with real exhaustion, he decided to stay up until his missive was completed, going into detail about what he had witnessed in Dover.

Once the task was complete, he pressed his seal—a hawk, symbolic of his code name, *the Hawk*, during his service as an agent of the Crown—into the wax, leaving behind its unmistaka-ble mark.

While he felt no closer to uncovering the identity of the Pied Piper, he had at least secured a convincing false identity—one he might need to use again without arousing suspicion.

More importantly, he had observed what could be the true source of Bridgewater's unease—and the man behind it all.

Baron Darkmoor. A man who raised more questions than he answered.

Too tired to bother with a proper bath, William used the water in the basin in his bedchamber and quickly went through his ablutions. He tugged off his clothes, leaving them in a heap for Patrick to deal with in the morning, and climbed beneath the covers of his bed. It was an unspoken agreement they'd made years ago: unless William specifically asked him to wait up, Patrick was free to retire with the rest of the household staff. Only the footmen and security guards assigned to patrol the estate and the manse worked through the night. Finally, with a deep sigh, William closed his eyes and let sleep claim him.

It didn't last long.

He was awakened by a piercing cry. Realizing it was Michael, William threw on his breeches and his dressing gown and rushed up to the nursery.

Mrs. Randal gently dabbed the boy's forehead with a damp cloth. "Sweetheart, it's me, Mrs. Randal. I'm right here with you. You're safe now—there's nothing and no one here to harm you."

Her pleas were having no effect. Michael continued to scream as loudly as he could as the night terror possessed him. "I want Mummy," the boy wailed, tossing his head from side to side.

"His night terrors are back, Mrs. Randal," William said. "I had hoped he was over them."

Michael thrashed beneath the sheets, his small body tangled in the linens soaked with his perspiration. His face was contorted in the throes of his nightmare, and a low, panicked cry escaped his lips.

"Mrs. Randal," William called softly, though his tone was edged with urgency. The older woman, already at the bedside, moved quickly to loosen the blankets twisted around the boy.

"We'll need to change these sheets, Mr. William," she said, as her hands worked to free Michael. "The poor child is drenched through."

William nodded as he helped her, his focus fixed on Michael, who flinched and mumbled incoherently, still trapped in the dream's grip. Kneeling beside the bed, William placed a firm but gentle hand on his brother's shoulder, speaking low and steady. "Michael, it's William. You're safe. Wake up, lad. I'm here."

But the boy's tremors didn't abate. His small fists curled tightly into the sheets, and his breathing remained shallow and ragged.

"We'll need to move him," Mrs. Randal said briskly, her voice betraying a hint of worry. She had already retrieved fresh bedding, her movements efficient despite the lateness of the hour.

"I'll take him," William said. Carefully, he slipped his arms under Michael's thin frame and lifted him, the boy's head lolling against his shoulder. Michael whimpered, weakly clutching at William's shirt as though he were reaching for something solid in the storm of his terror.

"Shh, it's all right, Michael," William murmured, cradling him close. "It's me. I won't let anything harm you."

Mrs. Randal quickly stripped the soaked sheets, her swift motions accompanied by the faint rustle of linen and the snap of fresh fabric being laid in place. All the while, William held the boy tightly, his hand smoothing over Michael's damp hair. The boy's body remained tense, and William could feel the tremors still rippling through him.

"It's over, Michael," he said again. "You're not alone. You're safe."

As Mrs. Randal finished remaking the bed, William settled Michael back onto the fresh sheets, keeping one hand on the boy's chest to ground him. Michael's breathing hitched, but slowly began to steady, the nightmare loosening its claws bit by bit.

Mrs. Randal tucked the blankets securely around him. "He'll sleep easier now, sir," she said, her tone more hopeful than certain.

William didn't leave, pulling a chair close to the bedside. "I'll stay with him," he said, his gaze never leaving Michael's face. "If the nightmare comes again, he won't face it alone."

The little boy opened his eyes and, looking at William, wailed for his mother. "Don't let them take Mummy," he said hoarsely in between big gulps of air.

"Michael, I'm here with you now. And I'm not going any-where," William insisted, pouring a cup of water and holding it to Michael's lips.

"William?" the little boy said after taking a few sips. "Can I stay with you tonight?" He hiccupped.

"Yes, sprout. We will talk about your bad dream tomorrow. But for tonight, you can sleep in my bed."

"My lord, is there anything I can do?" Patrick asked, rushing into the room a minute later, his face creased with concern.

"Just quickly prepare my room," William said. "I'm going to let Michael sleep in there this once, so everyone can get some rest."

Patrick hesitated a moment, his brows knitting in concern, but then gave a quick nod and hurried off to do as he was bidden.

By the time William carried Michael into his chamber, the valet had already worked his usual magic. The discarded clothing and scattered shoes had been cleared away, and the bed was freshly made. Patrick had even arranged a special area on the far side of the bed, piling extra pillows and blankets to create a comfortable, separate space for the boy.

"Very good, Patrick," William said quietly as he settled Mi-chael onto the prepared side of the bed. Michael stirred faintly, his small fingers clinging briefly to William's sleeve before relaxing again. The boy's exhaustion was palpable, though the occasional tremor from his nightmare still rippled through him. "I'm right here, Michael," William murmured, smoothing the blankets over the child. "You've nothing to fear now."

Patrick stood to one side, attentive but unobtrusive. "Shall I bring anything else, my lord?"

"No, Patrick. That'll be all for tonight," William replied, glancing up. "Thank you."

Patrick inclined his head and slipped out of the room, leaving William alone with his young charge. The room fell into a hushed stillness, broken only by the soft crackle of the fire in the hearth. William lowered himself onto the bed beside Michael, his presence offering a silent reassurance.

As the boy's breathing evened out, William leaned back, letting his head rest against the headboard. He knew the day's burdens wouldn't allow him much sleep, but at least Michael was calm—and that was all that mattered tonight.

William hoped he'd have the same good fortune. This was the second time this week that Michael had sought comfort this way. He couldn't sleep in here long term; William needed to find a way to help his brother face his fears and get through these episodes.

A FEW HOURS later, he was startled awake by the sharp sound of curtains being drawn back. Bright sunlight flooded the room, eliciting a groan from William as he turned his face into the pillow. After the long night he'd endured, his eyes felt gritty and irritated—almost as irritated as the rest of him. All he wanted was an hour or two more of precious sleep.

"What is it, Patrick? This had better be good," he grumbled, his voice thick with fatigue. He looked over where Michael had been just a few hours earlier, and the area was empty. "Wait. Where's Michael?"

"He woke up earlier, and I happened by and took him back to the nursery for breakfast," Patrick said. "My apologies, my lord, but you have another problem. Lady Bella Connolly has arrived. She told Harlow she wasn't expected, but said she had something important to discuss with you."

"Lady Bella… Here… Now?" William said, bolting upright so abruptly that he nearly tumbled out of bed. Scrambling to focus his bleary eyes, he fixed a questioning look on his valet. "What time is it?"

"It's almost noon, my lord."

"Damn," William muttered. "Help me dress, will you?"

"I live to serve, my lord," Patrick replied, his words carrying just enough sarcasm to earn him a raised brow. Nevertheless, he swiftly laid out William's buckskin trousers, a crisp shirt, and a neatly folded neckcloth.

William shot his valet a pointed look but didn't bother hiding his smirk. *Cheeky fellow.*

Fifteen minutes later, dressed and marginally more awake, William descended the stairs and made his way to the drawing room.

Pushing open the doors, he found Bella seated on the settee, flipping through a newspaper he'd left on the side table a few days ago. At her feet, Lacey lay curled up in a warm pool of sunlight, her tail occasionally twitching in contentment.

William paused for a moment, taking in the scene. Bella, as always, was a balm to his weary soul and, in this case, a sight for his sore, sleep-deprived eyes.

"Good day, Bella," he greeted her as he approached.

"Good day, William," she replied, looking up with a smile that seemed to illuminate the room. He resisted the urge to sigh again—this time from sheer admiration. Her beauty was a perfect blend of refreshing and breathtaking.

"Are you finished with this?" she asked, holding up the latest edition of the *Ton Tattler.*

"That old thing?" William chuckled. "It arrived a week ago. I suppose it's past its expiration date. Of course you may have it."

He had little patience for gossip and only read the *Tattler* out of necessity.

Bella grinned. "Oh, the gossip is entertaining, but I'm more interested in fashion. There are two lovely patterns on the second page."

"Well, I'm glad it's getting another life. I was about to toss it," he admitted.

"Happy to be of service," she said, her tone playful. "My grandmothers love gossip, even though they claim otherwise. They refuse to subscribe to the *Tattler*, but I've caught them reading over their friends' shoulders at the tearoom." She giggled. "Honestly, I don't know anyone who *doesn't* sneak a peek at it, no matter what they say. Even if most of it is probably nonsense, there's some value in it."

"I suppose so," William replied with a deep laugh, suddenly grateful he hadn't been featured in its pages—at least not to his knowledge. "I'll ask Harlow to see that the *Tattler* is delivered to you from now on—after I've had the chance to read through it, of course."

"Thank you, William. You are most kind," she said, her sunny smile bright enough to light the dimmest corners of his day.

How he yearned to kiss those radiant lips, to taste the warmth of that smile and claim it as his own. But he held himself in check, his hands curling at his sides as though restraint alone could tether the desire threatening to overwhelm him.

BELLA HAD TO keep reminding herself not to stare, though she could easily spend the entire day gazing at him without tiring. He was utterly captivating—a man seemingly oblivious to the effect his rugged, masculine beauty had on her, and undoubtedly on countless other women. She couldn't help but wonder how many hearts William had unknowingly—or perhaps knowingly—broken in the course of his work. With his golden waves of hair and those striking sky-blue eyes, it seemed inevitable.

Whenever she found herself this close to him, her breath caught in her throat, her chest felt impossibly tight, and her mouth was as dry as a parched desert. Good heavens, if she wasn't careful, she might very well swoon on the spot, reduced to little more than a hopelessly smitten fool in his presence.

"I understand you came to talk to me about something?" he said.

"I did," she said, clearing her throat. She had given a lot of thought to what Michael had told her the other day. Only she didn't want to go by herself. "Is Michael with his governess?" she blurted, without thinking.

He glanced at the light gold Ormolu clock on the mantel. "Michael's having riding lessons about now. The boy has probably been up for hours."

"I didn't know he was getting riding lessons," she said.

"I realized it was high time he learned how to ride," William admitted with a sheepish smile. "It's entirely my fault that it's taken this long."

"I'm pleased to hear that. I'm sure he'll pick it up quickly," she replied with a smile.

"Michael is a clever boy," he said with a chuckle. "And he's strong, too—much better at climbing trees than I ever was at his age."

The door opened, and Harlow stepped inside, followed by a footman pushing a cart. "My lord, I thought you might like some refreshment," he said with a deferential bow.

"Thank you, Harlow," William replied, offering his arm to Bella. "Shall we?"

She nodded, grateful for the prospect of tea to soothe her parched throat. As William busied himself with the tea, she thought she caught a faint whiff of something heavily floral and musky. It seemed out of place, clashing with the savory aroma of sandwiches, biscuits, and the fragrant tea Harlow had brought in. She dismissed it as her imagination—where would William have acquired such a scent, after all?

But as he settled into the chair across from her, the fragrance returned, stronger this time. It wasn't her imagination. The rich, heady scent clung to him like a second skin, unmistakably perfume. Her thoughts stumbled as she considered the possibilities. Surely it could not be a member of the female staff or Michael's governess. Had he been somewhere—perhaps *with* someone—whose scent now lingered on him?

The notion struck her like a physical blow, twisting in her gut. Had William taken a lover? The question gnawed at her, unwelcome and unsettling, as she forced herself to sip her tea and feign composure.

"What was it you needed to speak with me about? I doubt it was to ask me to share my *Ton Tattler* with you," he said, taking a bite of a sandwich.

She gave a forced laugh, suddenly unsure of what to say. "Uh… no. I wanted to ask…" She took a deep breath as the question stuck in her throat. The question had been important, but she couldn't ask him. Not now.

"Bella, I can see that you're upset, but I'm not sure I understand why," William said, leaning forward, his brow furrowed in genuine concern. "Have I said or done something to offend you?"

Her cheeks flushed as the heavy, unmistakably feminine fragrance lingered in the air between them, as though taunting her. Unable to hold back, she blurted, "Perhaps it's more about *where* you've been." Her voice trembled slightly, betraying the ache in her heart.

There was no official understanding between them—not yet—but the thought of him with another woman felt like a dagger twisting deep in her chest. She lowered her gaze, her emotions a tempest she couldn't quite hide.

"Where I've been?" He frowned, confused.

"Last night. It's clear you were out all night," she snapped, aware she was making a cake of herself. But she couldn't seem to stop.

The atmosphere between them grew thick with tension.

"You know where I've been? How?" he asked, his voice suddenly raspy.

How dare he treat me like some brainless girl? Anger bubbled up within her. "I may be young, but I'm not ignorant. I know you went to town last evening. And wherever you went, you still reeked of the cheap, tawdry perfume from your illicit rendezvous."

His confusion turned to shock, which only angered her more.

She stood abruptly. "I've changed my mind about my request for a favor." She glanced down at her slumbering dog. "Come, Lacey, we should take our leave." Fighting back tears, Bella held her head high as she strode from the room.

The dog growled at William before turning and trotting after her mistress out the door.

CHAPTER NINE

Three days later
Bridgewater Manor

B ELLA HADN'T SEEN William since she'd stormed out of his home three days ago. In that time, she'd attempted to approach his manor house on three separate occasions, only to turn back when she neared the manse. She had reflected on her behavior and her words and knew she needed to apologize. While she was uncertain about her feelings toward William, she knew it was the right thing to do. But despite making repeated efforts, she couldn't. *Why am I unable to make this right?*

Despite her love for Winterborne and her desire to ride the horse, she had refrained from doing so. For days Michael's comments had rolled around in her head... over and over until her head and heart hurt. Her lack of interaction with Winterborne had hurt the creature, and she wanted to fix things. Until Michael had mentioned it that day in the stables, Bella hadn't realized the extent of her distance. She wanted to ride Winterborne—she *really* did. And he needed to feel her companionship, something that he couldn't feel through his stall door, no matter how many carrots she fed him.

Between her behavior toward William and her neglect of Winterborne, she had much to make amends for. If there was one lesson her father had instilled in her, it was that a simple, heartfelt apology—offered promptly—could go a long way in setting things right.

Bella was an expert horsewoman, but since her father's death, nameless anxiety was keeping her back. Now, as she finally confronted her fear, she understood that she couldn't help Winterborne until she first found the strength to help herself. Determined to face her challenges, she'd decided to seek William's help. But instead of asking him to go riding with her, as she'd intended, she'd turned into the worst kind of harpy and accused him of having an illicit interlude with a woman. Her outburst was most presumptive, regrettable, and unforgettable. Shame heated her face at the thought of it.

Craving solitude to gather her thoughts, she had confined herself to her room, even taking her meals there. Both grand-mothers had visited individually and together, offering gentle inquiries about what was troubling her. Not wanting to burden them, she had brushed off their concern with a wobbly smile, claiming she was simply dealing with her monthlies and needed a bit of rest.

Perhaps she told herself this excuse was to spare them worry, but the truth was far less tidy. Whenever she dwelled on what she had done, shame washed over her like a tide she couldn't hold back. Pulling a pillow over her head, she would burst into tears, overwhelmed by mortification.

Neither she nor William had made any promises to each other. *He isn't even aware of my attraction to him.* And she was *very* attracted. Not only was he the most handsome man she had ever met, he was genuine and kind. And best of all, he made her laugh. Still, she couldn't seem to stop crying.

Bella tried to justify her behavior, but no matter how she framed it, she came up short. She thought back to that morning three days ago. When William had come downstairs, it was clear he'd slept in—his slightly tousled hair, drowsy eyes, and raspy voice all betraying the late night he must have had.

Her heart had fluttered at how effortlessly attractive he looked, and she couldn't stop the unbidden vision of him in his bed. *Lordy!* But when he had stepped closer to assist her to the table, the scent clinging to him told a different story. It was unmistakably feminine, hinting at a bordello or a lover's embrace. The realization had hit her like a blow—he must have returned so late that he hadn't even had time to bathe.

Though she had no right to judge his actions, she'd done it anyway—and the memory filled her with shame.

Shocked at the heady smell of the tawdry perfume, Bella had tried, convicted, and sentenced William without giving him a moment's chance to defend himself. What if there was an innocent answer? Between them, her grandmothers had offered up a dozen reasons to invite William and his adorable little brother over for tea... or visit Dover. But Bella had pleaded the megrims.

By the third morning, the situation with her grandmothers had reached a boiling point. They had begun threatening to send for the doctor—or worse, to ask the cook, Mrs. Bisque, to prepare her infamous, vile concoction. Bella shuddered. The last time she'd feigned illness, Grandmère had insisted the cook brew "the drink," a mysterious remedy that smelled so foul even pigs would have turned their noses up at it.

Bella knew her time was up. Either she confessed or she'd have to brace herself for the nauseating brew. Her grandmothers clearly saw through her fabricated malady, though they didn't understand the reason behind it. And now that she'd had time to reflect, Bella wasn't sure she understood it either.

What have I done? she wondered, the question weighing heavily on her chest.

There was nothing to do but visit Cliffton Abbey and undo the damage she had inflicted on her friend. She would have to put off her grandmothers a while longer and promise to tell them all after she returned.

Now that she'd come to a decision, she was anxious to see William. She missed him and still hoped to ask him to help her with Winterborne. But it was more than that. There was no one else who made her feel as safe as he did. He was the only person she felt comfortable having with her while riding her father's horse.

As she and Lacey stepped outside, she saw two horses cantering toward her—the smaller brown mare was going slower than the stallion, and there was a lead rope attached to the horse's reins.

"Lady Bella, look at me," Michael shouted. "I'm widing Daisy, my vewy own horse!"

"Michael… that's wonderful!" She applauded his achievement, genuinely happy for her young friend, setting aside her own problems as she approached them. She glanced at William, who was riding alongside Michael, but quickly diverted her gaze to the boy. "And what a wonderful name for a horse. I love it."

"I've been taking riding lessons," he said.

"That was very nice of your brother," she said, chancing another peek at William, who smiled down at Michael.

Lacey barked her approval and spun around as if to celebrate.

"Bella, we apologize for our sudden arrival, but there is something I would like to discuss with you," William said. "And I decided I wasn't going to put another day between us."

Eyes wide, Bella nibbled her bottom lip, unsure of what to say. "I'm sure we can speak in Grandmama's parlor," she said. She glanced from William to Michael.

"Do you think your footman would mind taking Michael's horse for a walk around your grounds?" William asked.

Bella nodded and turned to Albert, who was waiting behind them. "Albert, would you mind escorting Master Michael around the perimeter of the house?" she asked.

"Certainly, my lady," Albert said. Turning to Michael, he took the lead from William. "Young man, would you like to see the whole house?"

"That would be fun!" Michael said excitedly. "Can Lacey come with us?"

"Certainly." Albert looked at William. "My lord, I think I

have this in hand."

"Thank you," William said.

Bella led the way into the house and down the hall to the parlor. She stepped in ahead of him, and William turned to close the door behind them.

"I… I want to apologize for my outburst the other day," Bella said. "I had no right to say what I did."

"You said nothing that my valet didn't tell me five minutes later," William said with a sheepish grin. "I smelled terrible. "What did you call it… An illicit rendezvous?" He chuckled. "I rectified the situation of my questionable scent. But I need to explain what I was doing."

"N-no, you don't have to explain yourself to me—"

"Yes, I do," he interrupted. "I *want* to explain. The truth is… I met a colleague, someone I knew when I was working for the Crown, and he wanted to meet at a tavern in town, for anonymity purposes. In my line of work, in the past, meetings in such places offered greater protection. I know it sounds strange, but one can blend in easily in a dark tavern. But there was no tawdry perfume… at least not on purpose. Our discussion took longer than anticipated. But there was nothing illicit. I promise."

She believed him—at least the part about the perfume—which she was sure meant there was no woman. She had to wonder about this friend of his, though. Was William still working for the Crown? If so, was he engaged in something dangerous? She hoped not. She could not bear to think of him in peril.

"So, you forgive me?" he said with a charmingly crooked grin.

Bella felt her cheeks heat with a blush, and she glanced down at the carpet. "There is nothing to forgive, William," she said softly. "It is I who must apologize for what I said. It was rude and unlike me. I'm not sure why I spoke that way to you." She glanced up. "Please forgive me?"

"Of course," he said in a low voice.

"We're friends, still?" she blurted. *Lordy, I sound like a silly girl.*

"Yes. Of course we are."

She nodded, swallowing the sudden lump in her throat. She was *feeling* like a silly girl, too.

"Good! Because Baron Darkmoor's ball is in a week, and if I attend, I want to be certain I can count on a dance."

Her face heated. "O-of course. Yes. I would enjoy that very much. We are friends… are we not?"

"Yes. Yes, we are." He paused and then said, "Would I be out of line to ask what you had wanted to speak with me about?"

She was silent for a moment. Finally, she looked up and said, "I've thought a lot about what Michael said. He's very wise."

"Yes, he is rather insightful, especially with animals."

"Well, perhaps you… I mean, I wanted to ask you if you would ride with me. I haven't ridden Winterborne in such a long time, I've developed a…"

"Fear? I would think that is normal. I saw men go through the same type of thing during the war. Considering how your father died… I've been wondering, was there an investigation?"

Bella thought about it. "They ruled it accidental, but I don't recall any type of official investigation, other than the magistrate taking a look around where my father fell."

"I believe Michael is right. It would do Winterborne a world of good for you to ride him." He rubbed the back of his neck. "Do you still have your father's saddle and tack from that day?"

She wrinkled her brow and thought for a moment. "I heard a groom ask Uncle Stephen where to put it, but I never heard what he said. He was so distraught over my father's death—we all were—that it was more than any of us could handle. I suppose it was eventually forgotten. We were fortunate that Winterborne had no more than a simple sprain. Why do you ask?"

"I suppose I am merely being overly thorough. Just the hazards of many years working for the Crown. But would you mind if I examined it? Perhaps there is something that the magistrate may have overlooked. Or perhaps there was some logical reason for the horse to rear up as he did," he said, gazing into her eyes.

"That horse loves you—as I'm sure he loved your father. And if I can do anything to reassure you, before you take Winterborne out for a ride, that is what I would like to do for you."

"That is most kind of you, William. And yes, of course, you may look over the saddle and tack." She smiled. "So… is that a yes? You'll ride with me?"

"Yes. I would love to ride with you. But right now, I would like to do this," he said, pulling her close. He covered her lips with his. It was a slow and unhurried kiss, as if they had all the time in the world. Bella felt a sudden release of the tension that had coiled through her over the past few days, to be replaced by a rush of warmth.

Her senses were filled with the scent of him, sandalwood, citrus, and leather mingled together, and she relaxed into him, her arms curled around the back of his head, fingering his golden curls.

William's hands slid to her waist, steadying her, while the other lifted a strand of hair from her face and tucked it behind her ear. The world fell away as he kissed her again.

How many times had she dreamed of this moment? And now she was living it. William was kissing her. Her very first kiss. And it was glorious.

CHAPTER TEN

Bridgewater Manor
The day before the ball

THE LAST FIVE days had been filled with anticipation and joy. Bella and her grandmothers needed gowns for the Darkmoor ball, and shopping and fittings for the three of them had taken considerable time. There had been several fittings until, finally, the three women had everything they needed and were ready for the ball. It would be their official introduction to the local Society, and for reasons she couldn't understand, Uncle Stephen was adamant that she look her best.

William and Michael had visited several times. As it happened, William asked if she'd like to ride the afternoon after the ball, and she looked forward to it, feeling for various reasons that she needed it as much as Winterborne.

Whenever she had a spare moment, she spent it with the horse, including rubbing him down and brushing him. Occasionally, she took him for a walk with the groom or simply spent time with him while reading her favorite book from a corner in his stall, where one of the stable hands had placed a chair. They comforted each other with their presence.

"Darling, you have a visitor," Grandmère said, gliding into her room and shaking Bella from her reverie. A smile stretched across her face. "Your viscount is here."

Bella felt her heartbeat quicken like a drum in her chest, its rapid rhythm echoing the excitement coursing through her veins. A tingling rush swept over her each time she found herself in William's presence, sending delightful shivers down her spine. It was a sensation unlike any other, extending to a fluttering in her stomach that felt both intoxicating and unnerving, as if a swarm of butterflies had taken flight inside her. The world around her faded away, and all that mattered was the captivating spark between them whenever they were together.

"He's not *my* viscount," she said, as if saying it aloud would deny that every inch of her heart had already claimed him.

"You know what I mean." Her grandmother gave her a look of disbelief before tutting. "Don't give it another thought. Anne and I will entertain him until you are ready. He's a very handsome young man," Grandmère practically sang as she left the room.

"Grandmère!"

"What? I may be old, but I'm not blind! Now, hurry before Anna and I make fools of ourselves," she said, chortling as she closed the door.

Oh no! Bella glanced once more at herself in the mirror and winced. Her hair was in disarray, and she had only one pearl earring on. Fumbling for the jewelry box, she added the second earring. Then she quickly grabbed a brush, ran it through her tangled locks, and decided to leave them loose around her shoulders. After straightening her dress and taking one final glance at her reflection, she pinched her cheeks for a touch of color and hurried out of her room.

Leaving William alone with her grandmothers was a dangerous prospect. There was no telling what they might say to him. Still feeling awkward over her own outburst just days ago, she could only imagine the mortification she'd face if her grandmothers decided to meddle or speak too freely.

A few minutes later, Bella entered the parlor. Lacey trotted in behind her and curled up on the rug in front of the fireplace.

"My dear Bella, we've been entertaining your viscount,"

Viscountess Harrington said, her eyes twinkling. Bella felt her cheeks flame at her grandmother's words. She chanced a peek at William, who gave her a wink.

"Elise and I enjoyed our little chat," Countess Bridgewater added. Her gaze strayed to the bottom of Bella's skirts, and she smiled.

"As did I," William said with a charming smile. "Countess Bridgewater and Viscountess Harrington, I hope you will both save a dance for me at the ball," he added.

The two older women giggled like debutantes. "Most definitely," the viscountess said. "Consider it done. It will give me an excuse to wear one of those little dance cards on my wrist. Oh, Anna… How long has it been since we've done that?"

"Too long—since our weddings, I believe," Countess Bridgewater said in a cheeky tone. "I look forward to our dance, Lord Dudley."

Leaning over to her granddaughter, Grandmama whispered, "You have two different shoes on, my dear."

Bella blushed as she quickly adjusted her skirt to cover her shoes.

William turned to Bella as her grandmothers left the room, both women chatting excitedly about the finishing touches for their gowns. "Good morning, Bella. I wondered if you might have time to take a walk. And before I forget, Michael insisted on picking these Lenten roses, declaring that I should bring them to you," he said, handing Bella a bouquet that had been sitting on a side table.

"They're beautiful," she breathed. "The pale green color is lovely. Thank you, and please thank Michael for picking them." *Can I walk without drawing attention to my mismatched shoes?*

"I will," William said. "The color matches your eyes," he added in a soft voice.

Bella felt another blush heat her cheeks. She put the mismatched shoes out of her head. There was no way she would let an opportunity to spend time with William go over anything as silly as mismatched shoes.

Lord, I'm forever blushing when I'm around him. But she couldn't help it—each day her feelings for him deepened.

Her eyes fluttered closed as she inhaled the fragrance of the roses, letting her mind drift back to that unforgettable moment—her first kiss, one that replayed like a special melody in her heart. The kiss seemed plucked from the romantic pages of one of her favorite novels—a perfect blend of warmth, tenderness, and passion. It had taken Bella completely by surprise, and it had been completely unforgettable.

Every detail of his kiss replayed in her mind—the soft yet firm press of his lips, the scent of sandalwood and citrus that was a part of him, and the way his eyes had sparkled with mischief just before his lips met hers. It made her knees weak. She'd relived it at least a dozen times—upon waking each morning, and as she readied for bed each night. Even during meals, she often found her mind drifting to thoughts of William, which only made her shrewd grandmothers take notice and make teasing comments.

"Shall we go for our walk?" William said, offering her his arm. "I thought a stroll through your gardens would be enjoyable."

"Yes, that would be lovely," she replied. From the corner of her eye, she noticed Lacey stretching before trotting over to stand beside her. "I see Lacey is keen on joining us." She giggled.

"Lacey is always welcome," William said, crouching and petting the little black dog on her head.

"Although I'm not sure there are too many flowering plants in bloom at this time of year," Bella said. Her trips to the garden during the winter were limited to walking Lacey.

"I had assumed the same. So, imagine my surprise when Michael stumbled upon the Lenten roses flourishing in an unassuming garden tucked away behind the stables—a hidden gem waiting to be discovered."

She smiled up at him. "You could be right. We might discover some lovely blooms in our garden as well."

She accepted her dark rose pelisse from Garrett, who stood by the door, patiently waiting. She smiled her thanks at the thoughtful butler. Garrett had a knack for anticipating the needs of everyone in the household. She had learned long ago not to ask him *how* he knew things, because she suspected he also had a knack for listening at doors. She didn't mind, however, as the butler was a loyal member of the family and had been with the Bridgewater household her entire life. Everyone depended upon him… and his ability to anticipate and deliver what they needed.

Garrett strode ahead with his usual brisk efficiency, his posture as straight as a poker, and pulled open the door leading to the backyard gardens. "Enjoy yourselves, my lady, my lord. And… you as well, Lacey," he added, his voice stiff as he addressed the dog.

Lacey stopped in her tracks, lifting her head to give him a long, deliberate look—a look that could only be described as that of a regal queen—before trotting past him with her tail held high as if to remind him exactly who ruled the household.

Garrett's lips tightened ever so slightly, but he recovered quickly, stepping back to allow Bella and William to pass. Bella suppressed a laugh at the butler's obvious discomfort, while William smirked, clearly enjoying the interplay.

Lacey, seemingly entirely unbothered, made her way to her favorite spot beneath the jasmine bush, now in full bloom, its yellow flowers cascading like a cheerful carpet onto a neighboring dormant bush.

"You have jasmine for all seasons," William remarked, chuckling as he reached down to break off a small sprig of blossoms.

"Two years ago, before the wasting disease took her life, jasmine was my mother's favorite flower, so the second year Papa and I came here, we helped the gardener start the garden in remembrance," Bella said with a fond smile. "I enjoy the fragrance as well." She glanced around. "I had thought the garden wouldn't be as vivacious as it was in the spring, yet as often as I step out here with Lacey, this is the first time I've truly noticed the flowers blooming in the winter. It's been a long time since

I've heard the names, but I think those rose-like flowers are pink camellias—one of my father's favorites. Oh, and I notice we also have snowdrops and pansies." She glanced at the clutch of flowers in her hand and then pointed at a colorful patch in the corner of the garden. "Oh, and please tell Michael that we also have Lenten roses. I've never noticed them before."

"I'll have to ask our head gardener to freshen up the gardens around Cliffton Abbey. After seeing yours, I know we can do much better," William said.

They continued walking down one of the paths through the garden, both commenting on and admiring the varieties of pansies and other flowers the Bridgewater gardener had planted.

When they came to a bench, they slowed. "Would you like to sit down?" William asked.

What I'd like to do is kiss. "I'd love to," Bella said, taking a seat.

"Tomorrow is Darkmoor's ball. Your uncle will accompany you and your grandmothers, but I will be attending as well. And I hope to claim two dances with you, Bella," William said.

She brightened. "I'd like that. I'll save whatever dances you'd like."

"Then perhaps you would agree to the first waltz and the supper dance," William said, a teasing glint in his eyes as he winked.

Bella's heart fluttered, a delicious warmth spreading through her chest. "I'll make sure your name is on my card as soon as I arrive," she replied.

His gaze shifted to the lush greenery surrounding them. "These magnolia bushes are quite robust, don't you think?"

She glanced around, puzzled by his comment. "Indeed, they are," she said.

"They're so robust, in fact," he continued, his voice dropping slightly, "that they've made this bench quite private."

Realization dawned as her breath quickened. "Yes, it is rather private," she murmured, her cheeks warming as butterflies stirred in her stomach.

"I daresay," he said, leaning just slightly closer, "it might be safe to steal a kiss—if you are willing, that is."

Her breath caught, her pulse racing at his words. She hesitated. "I—I might not object," she replied, voice barely above a whisper.

William tucked the sprig of jasmine into her hair, then leaned down and covered her lips with his.

FROM THE SOLITUDE of his fourth-story bedchamber, behind heavy drapes that filtered the afternoon light, Viscount Stephen Bridgewater moved the curtain aside and stared at the young couple below. As he observed them, a pang of immense regret gripped his heart.

This is the man she desires and deserves. Yet I've set in motion something that I cannot stop and have saddled her with a man who isn't worth her notice.

Stephen's stomach churned at his dark thoughts, for he knew all too well that he had condemned his beloved niece to a life that would take her away from true happiness. Guilt washed over him as he recalled the slip of his tongue that had entangled his niece's future in that of Baron Darkmoor. The baron was now demanding a betrothal. And Stephen had no choice but to comply.

His late brother had always disagreed with his choices, but Miles had always loved Stephen, despite the reckless behavior that had defined Stephen's life. In a letter added as a codicil to his last will, the late earl had asked Stephen to take care of Bella and watch over her, should anything ever happen to him. Miles had trusted him with his daughter, even though Stephen didn't deserve the trust of anyone in his family. He was damaged—a wastrel, undeserving of anyone's trust or love, especially that of his brother and innocent niece.

Unable to think of a solution to his problems, he poured himself another brandy. At least he could forget his woes for a little while as he lost himself to the bottle once more.

CHAPTER ELEVEN

Darkmoor House
The night of the ball

B ELLA STEPPED ONTO the landing at the top of a grand staircase and gazed down into the ballroom as Lord Darkmoor's butler announced her family. She had not expected such elegance in Dover. The ballroom looked like something out of a dream—everything was large, bright, and sparkling.

Ornate chandeliers hung above the grand ballroom, their golden glow casting a warm radiance over an ivory-and-gold chamber. The gleaming onyx floor, inlaid with an intricate geometric design in hues of burnished gold, reflected the light like a polished mirror. Floor-to-ceiling windows, draped in sumptuous ivory silk with gold embroidery, framed the room, offering glimpses of the moonlit night beyond.

Amidst the swirl of elegantly attired guests, one figure stood apart. William—tall and striking, his broad shoulders carrying the cut of his midnight-black coat with effortless grace, the rich sapphire of his waistcoat lending a vibrant contrast. Golden curls framed his face, his smile as warm as the candlelight flickering above.

Bella's heart fluttered, an involuntary response to the sight of him. As if drawn by an unseen thread, he paused mid-conversation with an older couple and lifted his gaze. Their eyes met, and for a heartbeat, the crowded ballroom faded away.

Uncle Stephen, flanked by her grandmothers, descended the stairs ahead of her. As they neared the bottom, a dark-haired gentleman emerged from the crowd, his sleek hair neatly tied in a queue at the nape of his neck. With a deliberate step forward, he halted their progress.

Wearing a smile that didn't meet his dark, inscrutable black eyes, he exuded a predatory aura that sent a chill down Bella's spine.

"This must be your beautiful niece, whom I've heard so much about," he said smoothly.

Her uncle cleared his throat. "Allow me to introduce my niece, Lady Bella Connolly. Bella, this is our host, Baron Edgar Darkmoor. These lovely ladies are her grandmothers. My mother, Countess Anne Bridgewater, and Viscountess Elise Harrington."

Bella noticed his voice sounded raspy, and his eyes seemed to skitter about, but couldn't imagine why. Perhaps Society balls made him anxious?

The baron took Bella's hand and leaned over it, kissing her gloved fingers. "I am so very pleased to make your acquaintance, my lady. I hope you will allow me to reserve a dance." He reached for the small dance card dangling from her wrist. "Ah... I see I have lost the waltzes to another."

Uncle Stephen looked at her quizzically.

While the baron's voice was suave and warm, his eyes turned flinty as he perused the card. "Ah," he said. "Here, I found one of my favorite dances. They should play it soon. Unfortunately, it isn't the waltz, as I had hoped."

She considered herself lucky that she would not have to endure the intimacy of a waltz with the baron—for she had written William's name in its place. Though William had mentioned just yesterday that he wished to inscribe it himself, something had compelled her to do it instead, mere moments before they descended the stairs. The baron's very presence unsettled her, his demeanor leaving her with an undeniable sense of unease.

The baron shot a sharp look at her uncle, then, with a slick smile on his face, he turned to Bella's grandmothers. He took each of their gloved hands and kissed them, offering them a polished welcome. Bella breathed a sigh of relief when he finally moved on to greet a newly arrived earl and his wife.

"Who has already taken a dance, Bella?" Uncle Stephen hissed beneath his breath. "That was most awkward. We saw no one on the way in."

"Uncle, that's because he asked me yesterday for the dance. I promised to hold the spot for him, and I did," she said brightly.

"You are speaking of Lord Dudley?" His face wore a scowl.

"Did someone call my name?" William said, stepping up. "It's good to see you, Lord Bridgewater."

Her uncle's scowl quickly cleared as William shook his hand.

"Lady Bella, you are lovely as usual." He leaned over her gloved hand and kissed it, sending tiny, tickling pulses up her arm. "And ladies, you are both beautiful and charming," he said to her grandmothers, who both tittered like debutantes at their first ball.

Bella thought it amusing that her grandmothers had barely offered up half a smile between the two of them as the baron greeted them.

As the orchestra struck the first notes of the next set, a familiar melody drifted through the ballroom. William's lips curved in recognition. "I believe this is our dance," he said, offering his arm to Bella before guiding her onto the floor for the waltz.

Bella smiled up at him in anticipation as they walked to the middle of the dance floor. She noted several curious stares as he took her into his arms and began to twirl her around the room. As she relaxed in his arms, she spotted the baron's irritated face as he said something to her uncle. But William turned her too quickly for her to see Uncle Stephen's response.

Deciding to enjoy herself, she looked up into William's warm gaze, and her thoughts of the baron and her uncle faded. Even though they were surrounded by couples who were also dancing, it felt like it was just the two of them on the floor.

Despite having had dance and comportment lessons years ago prior to her debut, she hadn't attended very many balls during her two London Seasons. But dancing with William felt magical. His arms held her perfectly—his left hand firmly clasped her gloved right hand, and his right hand rested lightly on her back, just below her shoulder, while her left hand rested gently on his upper arm. His touch was light, yet he had no trouble whisking her effortlessly about the floor as if they had danced together many times before.

As they once more waltzed by her uncle, Bella noticed him leading a beautiful blonde woman in a deep sapphire-blue gown onto the floor. He glanced at Bella and smiled, warming her heart. She thought to herself that perhaps her uncle might find happiness after all.

Looking up, she met William's warm gaze again, and the old gypsy's prediction whispered through her thoughts. It had been only days since she and her grandmothers had visited the village, yet the fortune teller's words lingered. Could William truly be the man destined for her future? And if so, would he bring her happiness—or heartbreak?

DESPITE HIS OWN worries, Stephen felt relieved to see his niece dancing with Viscount Dudley. Pausing at the refreshment table, he studied the couple as they whirled across the floor. Even though Stephen was up to his eyeballs in debt to the baron, he disliked the man's possessive attitude toward his niece. Perhaps there was some connection to the nightmares he had been having lately. He grimaced, recalling the baron's irate conversation as he'd watched Dudley take his niece to the dance floor.

"How dare you spite me and have her dance card already claimed before I could place my name on it," the baron had ground out. *"I will have your niece as my wife, and you will not interfere."* He looked

across the dance floor. *"And neither will that sop, Dudley. I will have her inheritance. I will woo her for a week and then I will make the announcement."*

"You are a rich man and don't need her inheritance. Your home is ten times the size of Bridgewater Manor. And as I've explained to you, Baron Darkmoor, my niece plans to marry for love. I don't know who that will be, but unless she truly falls in love, she will not marry." He wasn't sure where his defense of Bella came from, but Stephen didn't back away from the statement, and for those few minutes, he felt good about himself.

The man glared at him. *"Enough. I will marry your niece, Bridgewater—with or without your blessing. And I will marry her before she turns of age to make her own financial decisions."*

What was it about Bella's inheritance that the baron wanted? Her father had purchased the manor house only a year before his death. Stephen recalled his brother saying it had been for sale for a year before they purchased it.

He'd struggled within himself. Part of him had wanted to smash his fist into the baron's face, and to hell with the consequences. But within moments, the weaker part of him won out. He'd simply nodded and made his way to the refreshment table. Stephen couldn't have felt more caught if his leg were in a bear trap.

"What does a woman have to do to gain a man's attention?" a woman beside him said now.

"You have merely to speak," Stephen said, turning. His easy smile faltered, and his heart jolted as recognition struck. The woman standing before him was as lovely as ever. How many times had he seen a stunning redhead—only to find out it wasn't the woman he'd hoped to see? Earlier, when he noticed a lovely, red-haired woman across the ballroom, he'd immediately discounted the possibility it was her. He had long since stopped hoping. Yet here she was, standing before him.

"Countess Elizabeth Rivers," he said, his voice touched with surprise. "It has been many years."

"Stephen." Her lips curved in a familiar smile. "It is good to see you again. You look well."

He let out a quiet, rueful laugh and shook his head. "I beg to differ. But you… you are as lovely as the last time I saw you."

Nearly a decade had passed since their last meeting, yet time had done little to diminish her beauty.

A delicate blush graced her cheeks. "Thank you. But time marches on for us all, does it not? We may no longer be in the first bloom of youth, but perhaps we are wiser for it."

Wiser. Stephen inwardly scoffed at the notion. He *should* be wiser, but his past was littered with mistakes. Mistakes that still haunted him. His late brother had possessed a clarity of mind, an inner peace he doubted he would ever attain.

"Er… may I get you a glass of champagne?"

"I was hoping for one… but later." She stared wistfully at the dance floor. "This is one of my favorite waltzes."

Realizing she wanted to dance, Stephen lit up. Elizabeth Rivers had been Lady Elizabeth Harrogate, a lovely and charming debutante in her first Season that Stephen had set out to court, only to lose her to Earl Rivers, due to a betrothal her father had made. She was still lovely and charming. If he were playing cards, he would have thought he'd found the ace of spades.

He held his arm out, and she took it. "Please allow me this dance," he said, forgetting about the drink he had needed only a minute or so before.

"I'd love to, Lord Bridgewater," she said, wearing a brilliant smile.

Stephen led her onto the dance floor, feeling more alive than he had in years. Her touch was almost ethereal, it was so light. And holding her throughout the waltz had him wondering if he was dreaming. Could he possibly believe in second chances?

WILLIAM HAD SENSED Bella's arrival even before the baron's butler announced the Bridgewater family. He'd turned, watching as she descended the stairs, her presence as familiar as it was captivating. From the moment he had met her—well, saved her from tumbling off the cliff's edge—she had occupied his thoughts. And in the days since, she had only deepened his fascination.

Yet he had tried to resist admitting what was now undeniable—he was utterly captivated by Lady Bella Connolly.

So, it was little wonder his temper had flared when he saw the baron making his way toward them, his gaze fixed on Bella like he were a wolf eyeing its prey.

"Good evening, baron," William had said as the baron approached.

"Viscount Dudley," the baron had returned in a brusque tone as he brushed by him, weaving through the throng of guests in his quest to get to the Bridgewater family. He'd seemed most determined to welcome them, pushing past other guests who were higher in status. William thought it odd at first, considering what he'd learned of the baron's desire to be accepted by the upper echelons of Society. He also noted that Bella's uncle had seemed... what? *Cowed* came to mind. At the time, William had been determined not to allow anything to mar his dance with Bella.

Then, when William had heard the man complain about Bella's dance card, it struck a possessive chord, spurring him to reach her side and whisk her away.

The exchange with the Earl of Bridgewater had been terse— and William had tucked his observation away to mull over later. Something about the two men didn't add up, he thought.

Returning Bella to her grandmothers, he decided that if the next two dances weren't too strenuous for the elderly ladies, he'd ask them each to participate.

"I enjoyed our dance, Bella," he said. "May I get you some refreshment?"

"Perhaps later. I see the baron crossing the room, and he

signed up for the next dance," she said. She smiled at William, but her eyes took on an anxious cast as she mentioned the baron having the next dance. "Although I look forward to our next waltz."

"As do I," he said, giving her hand a slight squeeze before depositing her next to Viscountess Harrington.

"My lady." The baron's slick voice oozed as he cut in front of William and claimed Bella's hand in a possessive grip. His fingers tightened just enough to make her flinch. "I believe this dance is mine." His cold black eyes flicked to William—just a brief, dismissive glance—before he turned his full attention back to Bella.

She hesitated, her fingers stiff in the baron's grasp, but with a carefully measured smile, she dipped her head and took his arm. Her movements were smooth, practiced, yet there was a shadow of reluctance in her gaze as they stepped onto the dance floor.

William exhaled slowly, forcing his fingers to unclench at his sides. The desire to rip Bella from the baron's grip burned hot in his chest, but he buried it beneath a mask of calm. Instead, he turned to her grandmothers with a courteous bow, schooling his expression into something lighter. "Would one of you lovely ladies care to dance?"

"We both would," Lady Harrington said, eyes twinkling. "However, I will go second. Anna, keep an eye on our girl. And isn't that the former Lady Elizabeth Harrogate? I thought your son would have married her, once upon a time," she whispered loudly.

"Yes… I also thought so at the time. But her father had other ideas and married her off to Earl Rivers," the countess said, accepting William's arm. "And look. They are dancing again, so this is the perfect opportunity to conduct a little motherly espionage."

William threw back his head and laughed. "I don't think anything gets past the two of you."

"No, it doesn't," the countess and viscountess agreed as one.

"Besides, I fear the mothers of all these young ladies will get their claws into this one." Lady Bridgewater smiled at William, "We'd have to do battle for our promised dance with this handsome man."

William laughed again. "I think we should hurry. The orchestra is warming up."

"As are we, my dear. As are we," the countess said.

CHAPTER TWELVE

As Bella and Lacey made their way downstairs to the dining room to break their fast, Bella's thoughts drifted to the ball. It was not an event she wished to repeat, and she had been relieved when the evening finally came to an end. Her feet still ached from the hours spent standing and dancing, but it was the baron who had left her most unsettled.

He had made a habit of appearing wherever she was. When she went to the refreshment table to fetch two glasses of lemonade for her grandmothers, he had suddenly materialized at her side, insisting that one of his footmen carry an entire pitcher instead. Later in the evening, as she stood by an open window, savoring the cool night air, he reappeared—too close for comfort—boasting about his estate and the many properties he owned.

By any standard, he was a handsome man, with broad shoulders, a patrician nose, white teeth, and thick black hair streaked with gray at the temples. He was older than her—by twelve, perhaps even fifteen years—but that was not what unsettled her. Despite his outward appeal, there was something about him that made her uneasy.

His eyes—so dark that pupil and iris seemed indistinguishable—held an intensity that made her feel watched, possessed. They looked soulless.

Even now, as she recalled the evening, a shudder ran through her. The man had an unnerving habit of materializing behind her—again and again—until it had begun to feel as though he were stalking her. He had insisted on two dances, his demeanor growing irritable when things did not go his way. His snide remarks and barely restrained temper had grated on her nerves. And when William had joined her for the supper dance, the baron had acted as if he had been personally affronted.

Thankfully, William had not backed down. He remained at her side, meeting the baron's dark glare with an unwavering presence, until at last, the man stalked off to claim his seat at the head of the table. She and William had taken seats as far away as possible.

At her feet, Lacey gave a soft huff, as if sensing her unease. Bella reached down to stroke the little dog's velvety ears, grateful for the comforting presence beside her.

"Darling, you're up later than usual this morning. Are you not feeling yourself? It's not like you to sleep so late," Grandmama said.

"I know, but last night was rather… wearying." Bella glanced around the table. "Where's Uncle Stephen?"

At her feet, Lacey nuzzled against her legs—a familiar tactic to earn extra rations of bacon or toast. If her grandmothers had noticed, and they almost certainly had, they chose to look the other way.

Grandmama grinned. "Your uncle had an appointment."

"I think it has something to do with the widow, Lady Rivers, he danced with at the ball," Grandmère interjected. "Three dances, they shared, including two waltzes!"

"I've heard she's a very nice woman," Bella said. "They seemed to be happy sharing time."

"Shh!" Grandmama chuckled good-naturedly. "We mustn't jinx it. But I confess, it would be nice to see my boy take an interest in something beyond his usual… appointments. The only person he seems to 'keep company with' here is that odious baron. I declare, I'm not certain what that man is up to, but I don't like that Stephen considers him a friend. Things looked tense between them at the ball last night. And I was concerned about his fixation with you, Bella. Every time I saw the baron, he was shadowing you or standing next to you. Very intrusive. And I understand he plans to call on our poor girl."

"You recall, we talked about how to handle that..." Grandmère said. "Remember?"

"I do… but Bella has a right to know," Grandmama returned, then sipped her tea.

"He plans to call on me?" Bella's stomach twisted at the thought. "I have no desire to accompany him anywhere. The man makes me most uneasy. His eyes… they're almost sinister," she said with a shudder.

"You handled him quite well last evening. I was watching—we were ready to jump in just in case. But your viscount handled him at dinner," Grandmère said, smiling as she speared a piece of her sweet bun with her fork.

"He's not my vis—Never mind," Bella said. She decided to eat while she let them discuss it. Over time, she learned there was more knowledge gained by listening. It gratified her to hear that her grandmothers felt similarly about the baron. Even more reassuring, they were actively devising some sort of plan to thwart the man's attention—something she very much wanted to hear more about. Bella feared he was the type to take what he wanted. But if it was her he wanted, then he would be sorely disappointed, because she refused to be taken!

"But you want him to be *your viscount*," Grandmama said. "I was not fortunate to have daughters, but I was a young girl once, dear. I can see the interest in your face… and his."

Bella was shocked to hear her relationship with William discussed so candidly. If he was interested in the future, wouldn't he mention that to her? So far, there had only been kisses. *Oh my God! Those glorious kisses.*

"Goodness! I nearly forgot—William will be here any moment," Bella exclaimed, seizing the opportunity to escape and avoid further conversation with her grandmothers. "We're going riding, and I thought it best to have a footman follow at a distance."

"Which horse will you be riding, my dear?" Grandmama asked.

"I thought I'd take Winterborne. I haven't ridden him in some time, and I'd like to make amends for my neglect," Bella replied.

"You've been in mourning. While a horse may not comprehend such things, any reasonable person would," Grandmère said gently.

"But my absence has affected Winterborne. I truly believe he feels and understands it," Bella insisted. "He was important to my father, Grandmère. I know it may sound strange, but I believe Father saw him as more than just a horse—he was a friend."

"Just be careful, my darling," Grandmama said warmly. "I believe your father would approve—and remember, you are an excellent horsewoman. You've been riding since you were barely out of leading strings."

The door swung open, and Garrett stepped in. Bella had noticed it before—an odd, simmering tension between him and Lacey that hadn't always been there. Once, she had adored him, wagging her tail and trotting eagerly to his side for a scratch. But now? Lacey barely deigned to acknowledge his existence.

As he entered, she lifted her head just enough to deliver a slow, deliberate glance—one of supreme canine disdain—before sighing with all the weight of the world and flopping back down, as if even looking at him were an exhausting inconvenience.

Bella narrowed her eyes. What on earth had happened between them? Had Garrett refused her a particularly good treat? Criticized her nap schedule? Whatever it was, Lacey clearly hadn't forgiven him, and judging by the butler's resigned expression, he knew it.

"My ladies," he said, approaching the table. "Lady Bella, a

missive arrived for you." He extended an arm with a salver. "The footman is waiting for a reply."

"Thank you," Bella said, accepting the note and quickly opening it. A few seconds later, she said, "It's from William. He said he would be here at noon for our ride." That was in two hours. She looked at Garrett. "Please tell the footman I'll be ready. Thank you, Garrett. Oh. There is one more thing. Can you have a footman meet me at the stables? I'll be riding Winterborne, and the viscount is accompanying me."

"Very good, my lady," the butler said, inclining his head and turning to leave, giving one more mysterious look at Lacey.

"I'M GLAD TODAY worked out for our ride," William said, lifting himself into the saddle of his gelding after he'd helped Bella onto Winterborne. This was probably going to be one of the toughest conversations he'd ever had—and having it with someone he cared about made it that much harder.

"Are we ready, sweet boy?" Bella said, leaning over the horse and petting him on his neck.

Winterborne whinnied, threw back his head, and nodded.

William laughed. "I suppose that's a yes."

"I think it is. Good boy," Bella said. Lacey barked as she ran alongside, and Bella stopped and slid down from the horse. Stooping down, she cradled Lacey's head and kissed it. "Lacey, not this time, girl. Keep an eye on everything at home. And please don't argue with Garrett—or maybe stay out of each other's way."

The dog yipped as if in agreement. William bit his bottom lip to keep from laughing.

Bella shook her head. "Go home, sweetheart. I'll see you later, and we can go for a walk." Once again, William helped her mount the horse before mounting his. As Winterborne began to trot, she glanced back at Lacey.

William saw the proud little dog heading back toward the barn with her head held high and couldn't help but be amused. "Let's take a slow start. I have a few things I need to talk with you about." He noticed the apprehension on Bella's face.

"I'm here and your captive audience," she said, with a faint smile.

Her hands trembled slightly, and William attributed it to anxiety from the long period she had gone without riding Winterborne. "It'll get better once we get started," he said softly. Although he knew discussing the death of her father would make things worse.

They rode in silence for several minutes, along the drive that took them to the main road that ran by both properties, before he finally said something. "I found your father's tack and saddle. It was left in the rear of the barn and had fallen behind a bale of hay. It was probably missed—and eventually forgotten about. It's just my opinion, but that's probably why it was still there."

Tears formed in her eyes. "Thank you for finding my father's saddle. I thought it was lost forever. When Winterborne was brought back, I looked for it, but it was gone. I suppose with all that had happened, I forgot about it."

"There's more," William said, hating what he was about to tell her. But she needed to know it wasn't the horse's fault. "There were sharp pieces of glass driven into the bottom of the saddle. The shards were so minute that no one would have noticed them. It's not a certainty, but there's a chance they were placed there on purpose. As the glass jutted through the blanket, it would have caused the horse pain. *Real pain.*"

"Oh God! Poor Winterborne. And my poor father. As they rode, it would have driven the glass into Winterborne's back." She blew out a breath. "Do you mind if we stop for a few minutes? I just need some time to think about this."

The footman who had been trailing them secured his horse and approached them. "Is there a problem, my lady? My lord?"

Wiping her eyes, she looked at the footman. "I'm sorry. This is the first time I've ridden Winterborne. I just needed a moment, Albert."

He nodded. "Very well, my lady. I'll get back to my horse."

"Thank you. I suppose I was more nervous than I had thought," she said, leaning into her horse's neck and nuzzling him. "I think we are better. Aren't we, Winterborne?"

The horse whinnied, as if reassuring her.

Once the footman had retreated, William said, "I know you want to look, but we don't need to do that. I checked Winterborne myself, and there were several small, healed puncture wounds beneath where his saddle sat. His hair covers the healed scars, and that's probably why you hadn't seen them when grooming him. There were only a few, and they were puncture wounds. I can only speculate on how they may have missed them—but since your father had a head injury, they must have decided that his fall had killed him. They didn't look any further."

After a long moment of silence, he looked at her. "What do you say we keep riding?" William asked. "I'm sorry I chose to tell you when I did. But you should know your father's horse did everything he could to keep from yielding to the pain. I'm certain of it. The nicks on his back were probably painful, but I think something else caused him to react. I'm not sure what, yet, but I'm going to keep looking."

Bella leaned over Winterborne and kissed his head, then patted his neck. "So, what do we do to find this person who did this terrible thing?" She swiped at her eyes. "It's been over a year. Is it too late?"

"I am looking into it. I'll need a little more time," he said. "I have contacts that will help me."

"I can't thank you enough, William. I truly appreciate your taking the time to investigate," Bella said, exhaling a deep breath. Then, with a sudden spark of energy, she added, "Do you feel like picking up the pace? I think Winterborne could use the exercise— and so could I."

Without waiting for a reply, she gave Winterborne his head and took off, the wind whipping through her hair.

William's heart pounded—not from the ride, but from the impish look Bella cast over her shoulder as they raced down the main road. He was once again reminded of how strong she was. Despite her sorrow over the loss of her father and the pain that Winterborne had suffered, she retained her spirit and warmth. Bella was not only beautiful, but she was the kind of woman who would make a wonderful wife for a lucky man. But could *he* be that man?

CHAPTER THIRTEEN

Early the next morning
Dover Beach, beneath a pier

S TEPHEN HAD HOPED last night would have ended differently. Attending Darkmoor's ball had been a dreaded obligation, yet, against all odds, he had enjoyed himself. And it was entirely because of the former Elizabeth Harrogate—the woman he had once wanted to marry.

Seeing her at the ball had caught him off guard. He had nearly forgotten that her home was in Kent. But the evening had unfolded like a dream from the moment they crossed paths. They danced, they talked, they laughed. And when the supper dance ended, fate had seated them across the table from each other, allowing the night to stretch just a little longer.

Something had happened after the ball—something important—but the details had slipped through his mind like water through his fingers. He should remember. He *needed* to remember. Yet here he was, waking beneath a short pier, the shattered remains of a gin bottle clutched in his hand, his head pounding with more than just drink.

Seeing *her* again had made him believe, if only for a fleeting moment, that his life could be different. That there might still be something worth salvaging. But now, the cold grip of reality pressed in—damp sand caked his face, his evening clothes hung in tattered ruin, and the tide lapped dangerously close. A dead crab clung absurdly to his trouser leg, a grotesque companion to his disgrace.

The baron. His niece. The future he was supposed to protect.

Guilt twisted in his gut, more suffocating than the weight of his sodden coat. He had drunk to forget—but what, exactly, had he done? And why couldn't he remember?

When Stephen first caught sight of the red-haired beauty across the ballroom, his pulse had faltered, his mind instinctively reaching for a hope he had long since learned to silence. It was never her. Not since she had married and left London.

And that night, he'd had no intention of approaching her.

He had watched from a careful distance, unwilling to invite old wounds to the surface. But then she had approached him.

At the refreshment table, she had been so lovely, so effortlessly charming, and in an instant, all his memories of her had come rushing back. He had been utterly unprepared. His heart had flipped in his chest, and before he could stop himself, his mind had conjured every long-buried dream he once held for them.

The soirees, the stolen kisses in moonlit gardens, the carriage rides and promenades in Hyde Park—every moment had led to the day he had asked to court her.

But her father had had other plans.

The abrupt announcement of her engagement to Earl Rivers had shattered everything. The rejection had taken its toll—not that it had been her fault. The fault had lain squarely with him and the way he handled disappointment.

Drinking. Gaming. Losing himself in vices that never truly numbed the ache.

And now, after all these years, she had sought him out. She had danced with him and dined with him. And he—fool that he was—had spent the rest of the evening watching her, imagining what might have been.

But what had happened after that?

Because now, he was here—beneath a pier, soaked to the bone, a broken bottle of gin in his grasp. And he couldn't remember.

"And look where you are now, Lord Bridgewater."

The words slurred off his tongue, thick with bitterness. He dragged a hand over his face, grains of sand clinging to his skin as he squinted against the morning light. The tide lapped at the shore, indifferent to his ruin.

He had achieved something he had never wanted, something he had never deserved—his brother's earldom. And yet here he was, sprawled upon a beach like a common drunkard, the weight of it all pressing down on him as heavily as the headache pounding behind his eyes. He scarcely recalled how he had ended up here. The night before was a blur of brandy and regret.

Elizabeth.

He had been reaching for a drink when he saw her again. And for once, he had hesitated. Not until after she had gone did he allow himself to drown his sorrows. He had asked if he might call upon her, and she had demurred, ever polite.

But he had pressed her.

"Come now, Lizzy. I only wish to spend some time with you."

She had hesitated, her voice laced with something too soft, too sorrowful. *"Stephen, I do not believe that would be wise."*

His brow furrowed. *"But why?"*

A faint, trembling smile curved her lips. *"We are friends, Stephen, and always will be."*

"I want more than friendship, Lizzy."

"I know." Her voice was barely above a whisper. *"And that is my fault. Seeing you again sent me back years, and I fear I allowed myself to be carried away."* She lowered her gaze. *"Forgive me."*

"Elizabeth, I—" He had stumbled over the words, his stomach twisting. *"I never asked... is there someone else?"*

A grimace. *"No, there is no one."* A long pause, then a breath drawn deep, as though she were bracing herself. *"But I am a widow, Stephen—long past my debut, yet my reputation still holds weight. I owe it to Edward's memory to keep his name unsullied."* Her voice had wavered then, and she had brushed away a tear before meeting his gaze with quiet resolve. *"And though I will not deny an attraction to you… you have allowed yourself to become a wastrel."*

The words had cut through him, sharper than any blade.

"Why did you let yourself fall so far?" she asked.

And then she had turned away, her gown whispering against the grass as she disappeared into the night.

His last memory had been of leaving the party and making his way home.

And yet here he was, waking on the shore like a man shipwrecked by his own vices.

He exhaled harshly, letting his head drop back against the sand.

"Well done, Bridgewater," he muttered to himself. "Bloody well done."

Looking up, Stephen saw the first hints of dawn breaking over the horizon. The sky was painted in muted shades of gray and gold, signaling the arrival of morning. Normally, he slept until noon, but today he had awakened in the open, sprawled on the cold sand. Soon, the streets would stir with life, and he needed to return to Bridgewater Manor before he was forced to explain the sorry state of his dress.

With a groan, he pushed himself upright, fumbling in his pocket. Relief swept through him as his fingers closed around his purse. At least he had the means for a hack. He muttered a half-hearted prayer of thanks before squinting against the light, his bleary eyes stinging from a night of drink, sand, and damp air.

As his vision cleared, he took in the familiar sight of large townhouses and more modest homes beyond the stone wall that separated the beach from the town. He had wandered these streets enough times to recognize the neighborhoods. How had he managed to land himself here?

Stephen exhaled sharply and dragged a hand through his disheveled hair. He needed to leave before someone of consequence spotted him—before his disgrace became common knowledge.

He braced himself against the wooden post beneath the pier, gathering what little strength he had left. With a deep breath, he forced himself upright. His first steps were unsteady, his legs protesting after a night spent in the cold, but he had done this before. Muscle memory carried him forward, his stride gradually finding its rhythm.

He followed a narrow path, the scent of salt and damp wood clinging to the morning air. Before long, he emerged at the edge of a familiar neighborhood—one he recognized instantly.

The town of Dover lay between the cliffs and the sea, with many of its prominent roads running parallel to the beach. At this early hour, the sun had wasted no time asserting its dominance in the sky, promising a bright day. Stephen struggled to find a cab. He needed to get home before too many people saw him. After opening the gate to the beach, he closed it behind him and stepped onto the sidewalk, its packed gravel crunching beneath his feet.

Staring at the homes ahead of him, he recalled a glimmer of memory from last night. When Elizabeth left the ball, he had hired a hackney to follow her. When she'd departed her carriage, he asked his driver to continue and drop him off near the Winking Mariner, where he'd indulged himself by drowning his woes in drink. At least, he thought, touching his purse, he hadn't gambled.

Lost in his thoughts, he found himself standing in front of the white stone fence to an elegant stone three-story townhouse. The home was surrounded by a garden thick with flowering bushes. As he stared at the front door, it opened, and he stood face to face with Elizabeth, who was holding a leash attached to a small, fluffy, copper-colored dog.

"Stephen, what are you doing out here?" she demanded as a liveried footman stepped out behind her.

"May we speak, Lizzy?" Stephen managed.

"My lady, do you require assistance?" the footman asked.

"Thank you, Mason," she said. "Lord Bridgewater is an old

friend." A pause, then, with quiet resolve, she added, "I should like to speak with him. I will be quite all right."

The footman nodded and stepped back, but remained outside, while she nudged her dog forward to where Stephen stood on the sidewalk. "I confess I, too, have questions, especially after seeing you in this shape. Oh, my goodness! Your hand. You're bleeding. Let me see to your cut."

"I'm b-bleeding?" he stammered, looking down at his hand with surprise. "I suppose I cut my hand at some point last night." He should have been embarrassed, but it was too late for that. He'd done all of this to himself.

She led him inside the house, handing her dog's leash to Mason, and asked Stephen to follow her. They walked down the hall to the kitchen at the back of the house. She opened a small cupboard and withdrew a box that contained a bottle along with other supplies, including strips of white cloth. "Mary, can you send a tray of biscuits and tea to my parlor?"

The cook nodded. "I'll be glad to do that, my lady."

In her parlor, Elizabeth motioned for him to sit in an armchair and lay his hand on the small table. "It'll be easier for me to take care of your hand if you are seated." Leaning over him, she cleaned the cut with the solution in the bottle, which made his eyes water. It smelled like vinegar and a few other things. Next, she spread a salve that smelled like honey and herbs over the cut, and finally, she wrapped his hand in several of the cloth bandages. He could smell her lavender scent and closed his eyes, wishing he could lose himself in it... in her. She was quick in her ministrations and, when she finished, sat in the chair across from him just as a maid entered with a tray of biscuits and tea, setting it on the table between them.

"Will that be all, milady?" the young maid asked.

"Yes. Thank you, Annabelle."

The maid dipped her head and left.

When they were alone, Elizabeth poured them each a cup of tea and finally spoke. "I'm concerned, Stephen. You came to my home, which means you must have followed me. There is more to this than meets the eye, here, and I'm asking you to tell me the truth. Why are you here?"

"You get right to the point, don't you? I had forgotten that about you, Lizzy," he said, using the nickname he'd had for her years ago. When she said nothing, he continued. "I'm here because I wanted to see you again, but you refused me."

"I did," she said.

"Why?" He began tapping his foot, a nervous habit he had when he overdrank.

"Why don't you take a sip of tea—it will help," she said softly as she lifted her cup to her lips. *Those luscious lips,* he thought distractedly.

He did as she said, and he did feel better, so he continued. "We spent hours interacting last evening. And then… it all ended."

"But I explained that to you," she returned.

He set his cup down and ran his hands through his hair. "You're right. I *am* a wastrel. And I've made a horrible mistake, and now my niece… my brother's child, a child I love, may pay the price."

"What do you mean? Maybe you should tell me more."

"I don't know why I'm telling you about this at all."

"Stephen, whatever you tell me will stay between us."

He believed her and began to talk. Thirty minutes later, he found himself talking of slipping up and telling Darkmoor about Bella inheriting the manor house from his brother. Something he should never have told anyone. "I'm in debt to him for twenty-five thousand pounds, and he's demanding that I betroth him to Bella," he said, placing his head in his hands.

She refilled his cup with more tea. "Drink your tea. And eat a biscuit. It will settle your stomach and help to clear your head."

Again, he followed her direction, and he did feel better.

"What you have told me saddens me, Stephen." Lizzy sighed and shook her head. "Rather than deal with your mistakes, you have placed the burden on your niece's shoulders. She will have to pay the price instead of you. That is not fair to your lovely niece. I had the pleasure of meeting her and your mother and Lady Harrington at the ball. From what I could see, Bella has feelings for Viscount Dudley."

Stephen swallowed the lump in his throat. Lizzy was right about what he was doing. He was behaving like a complete cad. A good-for-nothing bounder!

She reached out a slender hand and laid it over his. "Stephen, this isn't who you were—at least, not the young man I knew years ago. You must make this right."

"Lizzy, that's the thing. I don't know how. I'm trapped by my mistakes—the drinking, the gaming, the losses, and now, I'm failing my family." He closed his eyes, unable to look at the woman whom he'd once loved and lost, knowing he would most likely lose whatever respect she had for him.

"I will loan you the money, Stephen," she said. "I was left with more than I could spend in my lifetime."

"I appreciate your offer, but I cannot take your money," he said, shaking his head. "No... these are my mistakes. I need to make this right."

"You do, but it has to come from within you. Don't be ashamed to ask for help, Stephen. You are strong enough to do this. Lord Darkmoor can only have power over you if you concede it to him."

"I know that you are right in all of this," he said, sighing.

"I think, deep down, you know what you must do," she said softly, squeezing his hand.

He laid his other hand over hers and gently touched the smooth skin, as velvety soft as pressed powder. "What happened to us, Lizzy? I thought you had feelings for me once, long ago. My brother could have spoken to your father."

"So could you have," she said in a sad voice.

Ah, so that was it... She was right again. He'd been too volatile, too reactive to do what was right back then. It had been his downfall. Certainly, it had led him down a dark road of drinking, gaming, and wenching.

"You must accept it. The past is behind us," she said. "I try to find happiness in my present."

"That is so like the Lizzy I knew," he said, attempting to smile.

"I do care about you, Stephen. I had real feelings for you before I married Edward. He was a good man, my husband. We had a good life together. It was short, though. Ten years. The war took away so many good men. Even though Edward was an officer, he chose to fight with his men—and he died on the battlefield. And that is why, as I explained, I cannot sully his memory. He was very good to me," she said quietly.

"I understand." He finished his second cup of tea and set the empty cup on the saucer. "As for the issue with Bella, I will make this right. But I cannot take your money. If it's the last thing I do, I'll make it right."

She smiled, and he found himself mesmerized by her warm brown eyes, and the charming sprinkle of freckles scattered across her nose that had remained unchanged in all these years. Her red hair was just as vibrant and thick, and he longed to see it down and flowing across her shoulders. She looked almost the same as she had when she was a sweet young debutante at her first ball.

"Thank you, Lizzy. Just speaking to you has helped me immensely." He rose and offered his hand to assist her from her chair.

As she stood, he caught her gaze and found himself utterly captivated. The soft glow of candlelight illuminated her features, but it was not merely her beauty that held him spellbound—it was something deeper, something that stirred his very soul.

"May I kiss you?" His voice was low, almost rough with emotion.

She hesitated for the briefest moment before offering a slight nod.

He leaned down, his lips brushing hers in the lightest of

touches before he pulled back, his breath unsteady.

"You are exquisite, Lizzy. Not only in form but in spirit," he murmured. "I have never known another woman like you."

His fingers lingered against hers. "I will make you a promise," he said, his voice resolute. "The next time I kiss you, it will be under very different circumstances."

CHAPTER FOURTEEN

STEPHEN RETURNED TO Bridgewater Manor, his thoughts tangled in his conversation with Lizzy. At least she had not shunned him—a small mercy that warmed him despite the damp chill clinging to his still-wet clothes and hair. The morning was yet young, and rather than risk disturbing his family, he ascended to his bedchamber via the servants' stairway. More than that, he had no desire to be seen in his current state—his hair thick with sand, his wrinkled garments marred by dirt and blood, and the unmistakable scent of spirits clinging to him like a disreputable fog.

Reaching the upper landing, he swayed slightly, his balance unsteady, and collided with a framed painting—a sunrise over the sea, ironically one of his own youthful works. The impact sent a shudder through the panel behind it, and to his astonishment, a section of the wall shifted, creaking open to reveal a dark, narrow space beyond.

Startled, he stumbled back, steadying himself against the wall. "What in the world?" he murmured. Peering into the hidden passageway, he found it shrouded in darkness, and it was impossible to discern anything beyond the threshold.

He would have to return when sober and armed with a lantern. And perhaps a sturdier constitution.

Absently, he made a mental note to have a handrail installed.

If he had nearly taken a tumble, then surely the household staff, burdened with armfuls of linens or trays, might do the same. But for now, fatigue pressed down upon him, the lingering effects of his drinking binge sapping what little strength remained. With some effort, he located the hinge and eased the panel shut, telling himself he would investigate further once he had rested, and his wits were fully restored.

Stephen vaguely recalled his brother once mentioning hidden passageways, but the details eluded him. At the time, consumed by gambling debts and the haze of near-constant inebriation, such things had seemed of little consequence. Now, regret settled heavily upon him. He had taken too much for granted, assuming there would always be time to speak with Miles, explore the passageways together, and mend what had frayed between them.

A sharp pang lanced through his chest. The last time they had spoken, they had parted in anger.

When he reached his suite, he stumbled inside and closed the door. After stripping off his wet clothes, gritty with sand, he crawled into bed, hoping for a few hours of sleep. The cool, crisp sheets soothed the unrest in his mind. Letting out a deep sigh, he closed his eyes, surrendering to exhaustion. Yet echoes of his conversation with Lizzy lingered.

I meant what I promised… I will make amends. Bella should not have to suffer for my reprehensible behavior.

A dreamy sensation enveloped him, like the ebb and flow of a gentle tide, drawing him deeper into slumber.

"But will you?" a voice questioned.

Stephen recognized it instantly. *"Miles?"*

"I trusted you, Stephen," his brother's voice insisted.

"Miles, I promise to fix everything—I don't know how, but I will," Stephen vowed, his voice unsteady. Sweat beaded on his forehead. Despite their arguments, he had loved Miles—still loved him—and always yearned to be even half the man his brother was.

But how?

All he had ever done was drink and gamble, squandering both time and fortune. After Miles's sudden death, he had grappled with the desire to change, yet he had been lost—drowning in debts, shackled to men like Baron Darkmoor.

And now… Miles had returned. Incredibly, he was standing before him.

Stephen could not—*would not*—let him go. *"I need to ask for your forgiveness—for failing you… for failing Bella. I'm so sorry for the way we parted."* His breath hitched. *"Your death… this earldom… I would trade my own life if it meant bringing you back."*

Miles's voice softened. *"I know, little brother. And I have always loved you—then, now, and always. But for now, my daughter needs you."* His tone turned grave. *"If you do not help Bella, she will suffer for your indiscretions. And you promised to protect her. You know what must be done."*

Stephen swallowed hard. *"I know. I need to make things right. I've failed Bella. I've failed Mother. I've failed myself. But worst of all, I failed you."*

Miles regarded him with quiet understanding. *"I forgive you. I believe you will make amends."*

Stephen exhaled sharply. *"I'll try, Miles. I swear it."*

A knowing smile touched Miles's lips. *"Good. Now, there's something I want to show you."*

Stephen hesitated.

Miles shook his head with a faint smile. *"I've been watching over you, doing what I can to protect you. But we don't have much time."*

Reaching out, he placed a hand on Stephen's arm—cold, devoid of warmth. A chill seeped through Stephen, sending a shiver down his spine.

"Follow me."

Stephen saw himself following his brother as if observing from above, into the secret passageway he had only just discovered.

"Beneath this house, a treasure lies hidden… one that will not only aid you, Stephen, but will secure our family's future for generations to

come. Many stories surround this lost prize, and over the years, countless have sought it—only to fail, blinded by their own assumptions. You must look beyond what is expected, beyond what others have sought. If you do, you will be the one to uncover this treasure chest at last."

The two of them floated through turn after turn in the tunnels with the glow of Miles's spirit body lighting the way. *"Look,"* he said, gesturing ahead. *"These tunnels stretch far beneath the estate, a labyrinth of passages that extend to Viscount Dudley's land. You must find your way through them, Stephen—explore every turn, leave no stone unturned. Somewhere within lies the treasure."* His gaze locked onto Stephen's, steady and resolute. *"I cannot show you where it is—you must uncover it yourself."*

"But how?" Stephen asked. *"What do I have to do?"*

"You will figure that out. Be strong and be the man I always knew was beneath the veneer of self-doubt. You are an intelligent man, stronger than you think, Stephen, with much to offer your family. Be that man," his brother said. *"Be who we've always known you to be."*

"I have begun to see the light, Miles, but I fear it is too late."

"It is not too late. You were already on the right path, which is why I was able to come to you. But hurry, we are running out of time. I must take you back, so ask me what you will..."

There was still so much Stephen wanted—needed—to ask. He couldn't let his brother go. Not yet. *"I promise you... I will make this right. But first, I need to tell you what I should have told you long ago..."*

And then, at last, the words that had been locked inside his heart spilled free. His thoughts tumbled out in a rush—memories, regrets, unspoken emotions he had carried for too long.

They reminisced about their childhood, recalling stories that had them both chuckling. Then Stephen's voice grew softer as he recounted the time Miles had saved him from drowning in the pond at their family estate when he had been twelve. He remembered how, afterward, Miles—sixteen at the time—had taken it upon himself to teach him how to swim. *"That near-drowning has haunted my dreams since your death,"* Stephen admitted. *"It keeps replaying in my mind. Is there a message in it, Miles? I can't shake the feeling that I'm meant to understand something."*

Miles held his gaze, a knowing smile touching his lips. *"Only that we always watched out for one another."* His voice was gentle. *"Don't you remember? You did the same for me."*

A long-buried memory surfaced, striking Stephen with sudden clarity. A storm. A shattered branch. He had been sixteen when a brutal storm tore through the area, leaving a trail of destruction. The next morning, as they assessed the damage, a massive tree limb had cracked above where Miles stood—ready to crash down and crush him. Stephen had acted without thinking, shoving his brother out of the way just in time. The branch had splintered against the ground, mere inches from where Miles had been. It would have killed him. Stephen had forgotten—buried the memory beneath years of drinking, lost in anger and bitterness. But now, in the presence of his brother's spirit, it all came rushing back.

"Don't forget what we've spoken about," Miles bade him.

"I won't. I promise," Stephen said. *"But can't you stay longer?"*

His brother smiled and nodded. *"I have a little more time."*

Stephen relaxed and began to tell Miles about Elizabeth. He told him about the ball, about waking up drunk on the beach—all of it. How she listened to him without judging. By God, Stephen loved her, he realized. He'd loved her ten years ago, and then, when he lost her, he'd pushed those feelings away. But he loved her still.

"She'll be good for you," Miles said. *"I always thought you should have fought for her when her father announced the engagement with Earl Rivers, but sometimes things happen for a reason. Sometimes we have to lose something before we see its true value."*

"There is still so much I want to ask you, Miles."

"We are running out of time. I must bring you back, so ask me what you will..."

"I think of you every day, Miles. I miss you. And I'm sorry for the childish way I reacted when you were only trying to help me. I have so many regrets," Stephen said, his voice cracking with emotion.

Miles touched him gently on the shoulder, sending a comforting warmth through Stephen, which puzzled him, since his brother's earlier touch had been icy.

"I miss you too, Stephen… more than you know. But I trust that one day, we will meet again and speak as brothers do—with the ease and certainty of eternity."

Stephen cleared his throat. *"I promise to remember everything you've told me."*

"One more thing… the treasure is there, but it may not be what you expect." Miles's voice remained steady, though his form had begun to fade, dissolving like mist. *"You must go the rest of the way alone, but trust yourself—you will find what you seek."*

Stephen strained to hold on to the moment, but Miles was vanishing before his very eyes, his form growing fainter, slipping beyond reach.

"But there is one more thing… something you must know." Miles's voice, though distant, rang clear with urgency. *"My death was not an accident…"*

STEPHEN JOLTED AWAKE.

His valet was pushing open the dark green drapes to the windows, letting the bright sunlight stream into the chamber.

Stephen's heart pounded; his mind was clear.

He was stone-cold sober.

For the first time in years, he knew exactly what he had to do.

"The ladies are in the breakfast room, my lord. And your bath is ready."

"Good," Stephen said, stretching and drawing in a deep breath. Determination settled in his chest, solid as iron. "Let's make this quick. There's a great deal I need to see to today."

His gaze flicked toward the window, to the morning sky beyond.

"And by God, I will see everything done."

CHAPTER FIFTEEN

Later that morning

"GOOD MORNING, GRANDMAMA, Grandmère," Bella said as she stepped into the dining room. "Lord Dudley is accompanying me and Winterborne on a morning ride. Would you mind if Michael stayed with you both?"

"My goodness, no. He's a delightful boy," Grandmère said, pouring herself a cup of tea. She turned to Grandmama. "Isn't he delightful, Anne?"

"A lovely boy," Grandmama agreed with a smile. "We'll play Jackstraws or Cat's Cradle."

"Oh, do leave Lacey with us as well—she adores Michael, don't you, Lacey?" Grandmère winked at the small black dog, who responded with a soft whoof and a thump of her tail from her usual spot beside Bella's chair.

At that moment, Garrett entered the room. "Lady Bridgewater, Lord Dudley has arrived to see Lady Connolly, accompanied by young Master Michael."

"Perfect timing, Garrett," Lady Bridgewater said, gesturing for the footman to set two additional places at the table.

"Good morning, ladies. I see you're all early risers," William said as he stepped inside with his young brother.

"Please, join us for breakfast, William, Michael," Lady Bridgewater invited them.

William inclined his head in thanks and gestured for Michael to take the seat to Bella's left before making his way to the breakfast buffet.

A smile curved Bella's lips as she watched Lacey greet Michael. The boy grinned and bent down to scratch the little dog's head, whispering something to her as he did. Lacey wagged her tail before settling contentedly at his feet.

Bella knew exactly what her dog was after—treats. Michael had taken to slipping Lacey bits of bacon or sausage. She didn't mind, as he was careful, always offering small bites. Besides, she usually did the same. More than that, she was heartened to see the bond growing between them. With each passing day, both Michael and William were becoming part of their family.

Lacey had sensed what Winterborne had—the quiet warmth of a little boy's gentle heart.

She would always be grateful to Michael for opening her eyes to the truth—Winterborne was mourning and needed her.

As if reading her thoughts, Grandmère caught her eye and winked over the rim of her teacup. Then, after clearing her throat, she asked, "Where do you plan to ride today?"

William returned with a plate, setting it in front of Michael—a careful selection of scrambled eggs, sausage, and a small bowl of porridge drizzled with honey and apple slices. "We thought we'd ride across both properties and give Winterborne some proper exercise." Turning to Bella, he added, "Are you still up to riding him?"

"Yes, I'm looking forward to it," she said softly. Her gaze shifted to Michael. "Thanks to Michael's keen awareness, we realized Winterborne needed more attention, and to know he's still valued." She reached out, gently touching his hand. "I'm so grateful to you, Michael."

The boy beamed. "You're welcome, Lady Bella. I was happy to help you and Winterborne."

The door opened once more, admitting Uncle Stephen. "Hello, Master Michael. Good morning, Mother, Grandmère, Lord Dudley... and Bella."

Bella paused, studying her uncle. He looked different this morning. His shoulders were relaxed, his back straight, and for once, his eyes were clear—not bloodshot from sleepless nights and too much drink. The pinched, gray pallor that had clung to him for months was gone.

"Good morning, Stephen. It's nice to see you up and about," his mother said.

Stephen smiled, a warmth in his expression that Bella hadn't seen in a long time. "Mother, you are looking your usual lovely self this morning. I was thinking—there's a fête in town in a couple of days. I hoped we could all go." Pouring himself a cup of coffee, he took a seat across from William.

"Of course!" Grandmama exclaimed. "It had slipped my mind. We saw several broadsides in town last time we were there, didn't we, Elise?"

"Yes, indeed, dear Anne," Grandmère agreed, her eyes alight with excitement. "What fun! I can hardly wait."

Stephen chuckled. "There will surely be an archery contest, tests of strength, and games for the children," he said with a wink at Michael. "Not to mention an abundance of savory and sweet delicacies. Tradesmen and women will be eager to display their wares, from ironworks to the latest French fashions. They've expanded the fête this year—it should attract even more visitors from neighboring towns and villages." He took a sip of his coffee, then made a face. "Ugh. I forgot the sugar. Bella, be a love and pass it to me."

Bella slid the sugar bowl toward him, but her mind whirled. What in the world had come over her uncle today? He was nothing like the man who had escorted her to the ball just days ago. Though curiosity burned within her, she was simply grateful for the change.

As Stephen smiled warmly at her, she caught a flicker of something in his eyes—a familiar twinkle. The resemblance between him and her father had always been strong, but now it was more than physical. For the first time in years, Uncle Stephen carried the same lighthearted spirit her father once had.

"I am certain my Roma friend, Madame Vorest, the fortune teller, will be there as well," Grandmère added with an enthusiastic bounce in her chair.

A shiver skittered down Bella's spine. *Madame Vorest.* The memory of their recent encounter sent a whisper of unease through her. The woman's cryptic vision still echoed in her mind.

There will be great danger… she had said. Yet she had also spoken of a great love.

Bella's gaze flickered across the table to William. Could he have been in Madame Vorest's thoughts? A thrill of excitement stirred within her. Though the warning of danger lingered at the edges of her mind, she found herself more drawn to the tantalizing possibility of what her future might hold. She peeked at William from beneath her long lashes, her anticipation curling in her chest.

Uncle Stephen cleared his throat, pulling Bella from her reverie. She blinked, refocusing on the conversation just as his expression turned serious. "Lord Dudley, might we have a word in private?"

William's brow furrowed ever so slightly—the only indication that he might have been caught off guard. Setting down his coffee, he met Stephen's gaze.

"I'd be glad to, Lord Bridgewater," he said, his tone respectful but edged with curiosity.

Stephen waved a hand dismissively. "Please, call me Stephen. After all, you are among friends here." His voice was warm, but there was an unmistakable weight behind his words. Draining the last of his coffee, he rose from his chair.

"We can speak in my study." He glanced toward Bella and her grandmothers as he prepared to leave. "Ladies, if you'll excuse us for a few moments—I have an important matter to discuss with William."

"Of course, Stephen," the dowager countess said, her tone mild, though her eyes held a flicker of curiosity.

The same curiosity that stirred in Bella. What could her uncle possibly need to discuss with William?

"Let us consider our plans for the fête," Grandmère said. "I suggest we aim to leave around ten of the clock."

"I like that idea," Grandmama agreed, with a nod. "Bella, what say you?"

"Yes, that suits me perfectly," Bella said. The thought of spending the day enjoying the festivities outdoors sparked a sense of anticipation around the table, including Michael and even Lacey.

"I can't wait to find out more about the pirate's treasure," said Michael as he slipped Lacey a rasher of bacon beneath the table—and not realizing all three women were smiling as he did it.

"I want to search for gifts we can give the staff on Boxing Day," Grandmama said. "I know it's still a few months away, but with so many stalls, there's sure to be plenty on offer."

"I agree—we're bound to find some lovely things," Grandmère said. "And I'm hoping to find a hat to match my new Christmas Day gown. I had it made just before we left London, and I'd hate to return simply to commission a hat before I can wear it properly."

Bella, her grandmothers, and Michael were chatting about their plans at the fête later in the week when Stephen and William returned to the dining room.

William's face looked serious, but his tone was even. "Thank you, Stephen. I will keep all of it in mind and appreciate your taking me into your confidence." His face relaxed as he turned to Bella. "I think we should be on our way, if we want to enjoy as much of the sunlight as we can today. I've asked Franklin, my footman, to accompany us. I hope that is fine with you?"

"Of course." Bella stood, a broad smile stretched across her face. She had always loved riding and was looking forward to taking Winterborne out again, with William by her side. His support meant everything to her.

He furrowed his brow as he looked at his younger brother. Michael was wiping bacon grease on his trousers from the rasher of bacon he had just handed Lacey. "Michael, you promised to be on your best behavior if I left you with your...*grandmothers.*"

The two women chuckled. "We will take good care of young Michael. He's such a dear," Grandmama said.

Michael grinned at his two adopted grandmothers.

Leaning down, William playfully tousled his brother's hair and brushed a kiss on his head. "Don't get into any trouble," he warned good-humoredly.

"I pwomise!" Michael said.

STEPHEN WATCHED HIS niece and William leave before turning to his mother. "Mother, could you spare a few moments? There are some things I need to discuss with you as well."

"Michael, what do you think about helping me choose where to put a new flowerbed in the garden?" Grandmère said. "I wanted to plant some flowers that were Bella's mother's favorites. And I know you'll be a great help."

"I'd be happy to help you, Gwand-mare," Michael said. "Can Lacey come?"

"Oh, yes. I wouldn't think of planting without her suggestions." She giggled. "Besides, I think it's time for Lacey to have a visit to her favorite trees and bushes."

Lady Harrington smiled as she ushered Michael and Lacey out the door.

"May we speak in your parlor?" Stephen asked. "It will be more private."

As they entered the parlor, his mother turned to him. "Stephen, you've been very mysterious this morning. What's this all about?"

"Mother, I need to tell you something heavy on my mind for

months. It concerns Lord… Baron Darkmoor."

"This sounds serious, son. Tell me how I can help," she said, sitting down and giving him her complete attention.

"It's bad, Mother." He combed his hands through his hair. "I have been gambling and drinking… and it's been going on for a long time. The last time I spoke with Miles, our conversation ended with angry and bitter words exchanged. And I have regretted that every day since his passing. But despite my sorrow over Miles's sudden death, I just couldn't seem to stop gambling." Stephen tried to quell his tense nerves. It was as if his entire body wanted to be rid of the burden of keeping everything inside. He heaved a deep breath, trying to pace himself. He did not want to overwhelm his poor mother—she had already gone through enough.

Carefully and methodically, he confessed all to his mother, who listened with quiet patience.

"Darkmoor has all but cleaned me out. I never win a game. The more I lose, the more I keep playing, and the more I keep playing, the more my debts pile up…"

"Please continue," she said.

"Mother, my gambling has reached the level of a ruinous vice. It is like a heinous disease that has infiltrated my mind." He wrung his hands. "I keep thinking that with the next game of cards or the next toss of the dice, I will be able to pay off my debts, but it's never worked out that way." Stephen hung his head.

"How much, son?" she asked gently. "How much do you owe?"

"I owe him twenty-five thousand pounds. But there's more."

"That's a lot of money," she said.

He exhaled a long breath. "Yes, it is. And it's not just money that he thinks I owe him. He wants Bella."

"What?"

"Somehow, when I was in my cups, I revealed how Bella inherits this house on her twenty-first birthday, which is not long from now. The baron has been pressing for a union, and now he's going to force an engagement—as a down payment for all the money I owe him. He plans to marry Bella, no matter what I say. That lovely young woman who has been through so much, losing both her parents at such a young age. Even though I protested and have tried to dissuade him, he refuses to back down."

"Well, it is completely out of the question," she said adamantly. "Baron Darkmoor is a vile man. I can see it in his eyes. And make no mistake, I saw the way he looked at Bella at the ball. Like a wolf eyeing its next meal."

"And Lord Dudley cares for her," Stephen said. "I realize that now. He is a good man."

"He certainly is," his mother agreed. "William would make a fine husband for Bella."

"I know," Stephen said. "Can you believe that I gave thought to asking him to whisk her away to Gretna Green?" He shook his head in despair. "My God! This isn't how the man charged with caring for his dead brother's child should take care of her."

"Is that what you spoke with William about?" she asked, her voice faint.

"No. I may have thought it, but I would never ask him to do so… I could never do that to my niece. She wants to marry for love, like you and Papa, and like her parents." He sat down and rested his head in his hands. Without looking up, he continued. "I thought the baron would have an apoplectic seizure at the ball when he watched Bella dance with Lord Dudley. He was furious. I refuse to let that devil of a man marry my niece, but what can I do to stop him? I am in debt to him up to my ears. Believe me, I've been trying to find an answer. But the man is like a dog with a bone."

"What if we pay him off?" his mother said suddenly. "If we pay off all of the debt, then he cannot force the issue with Bella, and you will be free of him. That's the answer. And I have enough money to do it."

"No, Mother. I must deal with this." Stephen felt the tension leave his body. He had no more secrets—and he planned to get rid of the baron's threat, somehow. But he could not take all that money from his mother. William had also offered to help. Just knowing that family and friends were willing to help him gave him a surge of strength he had not experienced in years. "There's more." His lips curved up in a crooked smile. "I feel hope for the first time in my life." He told her about Elizabeth. "I plan to ask if I may escort her to the fête."

"Oh, Stephen," his mother said, her eyes shining with unshed tears. "Lady Elizabeth Rivers is a wonderful woman. I always thought she would have been perfect for you. I still do."

"Thank you, Mother. Lizzy is indeed quite special."

"Stephen, for the first time in a very long time, you have spoken to me from the heart. Instead of giving me excuses, you have given me an explanation. You have given me the truth. I'm proud of you. I believe in you. Please, let me help you."

"I can't take your money, Mother." He reached for her hands and held them in his. "I am trying to be the kind of man Miles was. The kind of man he wanted me to be."

"Consider it a loan. You have so many gifts that you have yet to discover, my son. I want you to know that if you ever doubted my love for you, if you ever thought I loved Miles more than you, you were mistaken. I have always loved both of my sons equally. I want you to do well, Stephen."

"Thank you, Mother," he said in a ragged voice, wrapping his arms around her frail shoulders. "What you are doing for me... I won't let you down. I give you my word as a gentleman. I promise I'm giving all of this up."

"We must hurry and get this done. I want that horrid man out of our lives as quickly as possible," Lady Bridgewater said. "I'll give you a draft. This money is just sitting in the bank when it can help you... help all of us." She went to her desk and withdrew a box. From it, she took out a piece of paper and began to fill it out. "Here," she said, handing him the draft for the full twenty-five thousand pounds. "When you give this to him, insist on a witnessed letter confirming the debt is settled, with a reliable witness present. That way, he cannot dispute it later. Do you think he'll have your vowels on him?"

Stephen chuckled. "How do you know what a vowel is?"

His mother smiled. "Son, women know what happens beyond the framework of their homes. And we read. A lot. And I can assure you, we understand a great deal more than you think—"

The door to the parlor suddenly flew open and slammed against the wall, startling both Stephen and his mother, who turned to see the very man they were discussing storm into the room, followed by a harried and breathless Garrett.

"Forgive me, my lord, my lady. Baron Darkmoor insisted on making his presence known when I tried to explain you were occupied."

Darkmoor stood in front of the two of them, his hands on his hips and his chest heaving.

"Thank you, Garrett, it is quite all right," Stephen said, his initial surprise having faded, replaced by fury at Darkmoor's arrogance.

Garrett bobbed his head and backed out of the room.

"Whatever you have to say, you can say in front of my mother," Stephen said in a firm tone.

"It's time to pay the piper!" Darkmoor bellowed, pointing at Stephen.

"My son doesn't owe you anything after today." Lady Bridgewater reached for the draft from Stephen's hand and handed it to the baron. "This debt is paid. In full!" she said, her voice steely calm. "And don't think of lying about having received the full payment. I am here to witness it! And I have already written to my solicitors with all the details concerning this payment to you."

Stephen bit back a smile at his mother's fib. She had not had time to do that yet, but he knew she would do it as soon as Darkmoor left.

Now it was the baron's turn to appear startled. But he seemed to recover his surprise as his dark glare locked onto the two of them, an ember of fury flickering in his eyes. "This isn't over." His voice dripped with disdain as he turned and stomped from the room.

Stephen drew his mother close, enveloping her in a calming hug.

"Oh, what a horrible man," she whispered. "I'm so glad you finally confided in me, Stephen."

Before he could muster a response, Michael and Grandmère rushed into the room, followed by Lacey.

"What's wrong?" Michael asked, glancing around. "Someone very evil was just here. But I think he's gone."

Lady Bridgewater held her hand out to Michael, who walked to her and looked at her with solemn eyes. "You are an intuitive child," she murmured, embracing the boy. "And a charmer."

"Were you listening at the door?" Stephen asked, half joking, his lips twitching.

"Of course," Michael replied, causing Stephen and the ladies to burst into laughter. Even Lacey sensed the change in mood and began to bark and frolic about the room.

Stephen looked at the boy, whose bright blue eyes were sparkling with mischief. "I recall hearing that you enjoy treasure hunts. How would you feel about helping me search for treasure?"

"A real *tweasure*?"

"Yes!" Stephen replied.

"Oh boy! I love tweasure hunts. That would be good fun. Only… can Lacey come?"

CHAPTER SIXTEEN

"**D**O YOU WANT to walk a little before we ride?" William asked, hoping Bella felt as he did and would opt for time to talk. He hadn't had a chance to speak with her that morning, and there was so much in his head after speaking with Stephen that he wanted a chance to comb through it.

"I'd like that. Besides, Winterborne appreciates going for a walk beyond the stable yard for the first time in too many months. I can tell he's enjoying snacking on dandelions and other vegetation he fancies."

"If I didn't know better, I would say your horse is grinning. Winterborne seems to agree with you," William said.

"He's much happier, I think." She reached up and kissed the horse on the nose. "Winterborne, you're enjoying yourself, aren't you?" she asked.

The horse answered with a whinny.

"I have a question I must ask. And since we are alone, this is the first time I've had a chance to ask, but I've noticed the tension between Lacey and your butler, Garrett. What's that about?" William asked, a wide grin on his face.

"Oh, that," Bella said, holding a hand over her mouth to hide her smile. "Lacey stole food for Winterborne, and he stopped her the last time he caught her in the kitchen. Apples and carrots kept disappearing, and Mrs. Bisque, our cook, mentioned the missing food and teased him about taking it. Garrett is very proper and didn't appreciate being accused, even if it was in jest. He took it upon himself to find the culprit and hid in the pantry, only to discover it was Lacey."

William guffawed. "That's funny. She's holding a grudge! Did he scold her? Is that why she's being so huffy around him?"

"Yes, I'm afraid so. Garrett, who is the soul of patience, lost his temper at her, and Lacey hasn't forgiven him. She is a very clever dog, and very loving, but I believe she feels insulted by the scolding, and it seems she has a long memory," Bella said, her smile wide. "I'm hoping it resolves itself. They used to be such chums."

"If it continues, perhaps we can explore some ideas." William cleared his throat. "Speaking of exploring, there's an area I haven't explored yet," he said, pointing to a field of lavender in an area near the edge of the property. "There's a big, flat rock I spotted a few days ago, perfect for a picnic. And it just so happens I've brought a picnic." He smiled, tapping the basket attached to the back of his horse.

"But we can't eat in front of Franklin," Bella said. "It wouldn't be fair."

"Don't worry. He has a basket, too." William felt his heart do a series of backflips. Bella was not only the prettiest lass he'd ever met, but she was also the sweetest. Her concern was always for others. He'd be hard-pressed to find many young ladies in the *ton* who were so considerate and attuned to other people's needs.

Suddenly, Winterborne reared up, yanking Bella backward. She cried out and stumbled, her balance faltering as the horse lunged, grabbing her cape with his teeth and trying to drag her away.

In a flash, William shot forward, reaching for Bella's hand to keep her from falling as he caught the horse's reins and assessed what was going on. Winterborne's behavior was wild, but not aggressive—urgent, almost desperate. His muscles were taut, his ears pinned back, his nostrils flaring as he tossed his head.

Something was wrong.

After William made certain that Bella was steady on her feet, he turned toward the still-agitated horse. And that was when he saw it.

The steel jaws of an animal trap, half buried in the underbrush, glinted in the morning light.

A chill ran through him. Winterborne had been trying to *save* Bella.

His breath tightened as he turned back to Bella. Her face was pale, her eyes wide with lingering fear. Without thinking, he pulled her close, feeling the frantic rhythm of her heart against his chest.

Tilting her chin up, he kissed her—firm yet gentle, grounding them both in the warmth of the moment. The scent of her—wildflowers and something purely Bella—wrapped around him, pushing back the icy grip of fear.

"I've got you, Bella," he soothed, pressing a kiss to her cheek, holding her close.

She sagged slightly against him, her heartbeat slowing, her body softening in his arms. He didn't want to let her go. Not yet. Maybe not ever.

Franklin caught up to them, reaching for Winterborne's reins.

"Stay behind me," William said to Bella before turning to help steady the horse. Together, he and Franklin worked to soothe him, stroking his neck and murmuring reassurances.

Just as Bella started to walk back toward them, Winterborne snorted and pawed the ground again, his head thrashing, his agitation flaring once more.

William tensed, watching the horse, and then—he saw it. Another trap.

"Wait. Bella, don't move. Nobody moves," he said sharply, his chest tightening with realization. "We've misjudged Winterborne."

Bella froze, color draining from her face. "What do you mean?"

William ran a hand down the horse's neck. "My God… I see it too, boy." He looked around, spotting what he needed. "Stay here, both of you. Don't move a hair."

He strode purposefully but carefully to the nearest tree and picked up a fallen branch. Returning to the spot just ahead of Winterborne, he extended the thicker end of the branch and pressed it down into the undergrowth.

A sharp snap cracked the air as the steel jaws of the second animal trap slammed shut around the wood. Then he walked to the first trap and sprang it. *I thought we had gotten all of these,* he thought. *Now… two so close together.*

William exhaled heavily. "Winterborne sensed the traps before we did. He was protecting you, Bella. If either of you had stepped on one…" He didn't finish. He didn't have to.

Winterborne lifted his head, his ears twitching, then gently pawed the ground—calmer now, as if confirming his success.

Bella turned to her horse, her eyes brimming with tears. Reaching up, she cradled his face in her hands, pressing a kiss between his eyes. "I am so sorry, sweet Winterborne. Thank you for saving me… I love you."

The horse nickered softly, nudging her, as if to say he already knew.

William fought to keep emotion from his face, hearing the words he suddenly longed to hear from Bella—but they were for the horse, not him. How could he be jealous of a horse? A horse who had just saved Bella from serious injury, he reminded himself.

Suddenly, things clicked in his mind. "I'm no farrier, and it's hard to understand people at times, let alone animals, but I think what Winterborne did—saving you—he would have done for your father."

"He would've done anything for Papa. He would have given his life, I'm certain of it," Bella said, looking into the horse's eyes. "Winterborne, forgive me for the way I've treated you—not riding you, leaving you in the stable," she said, her eyes filling with tears.

The horse replied by softly whinnying and nuzzling her ear, making her chuckle through her tears.

"Think about how much Winterborne must have loved your father," William said, his voice low, steady—though his pulse was anything but. "Just now, he dragged you back to save you from a trap, right in your path. If you'd stepped on either one of them, it would have surely been sprung."

A shudder ran through him. My God, a trap could have severed her foot.

The image—Bella crying out in pain, the jagged steel clamping down—flashed through his mind, swift and brutal.

He could barely stomach it.

It was too horrible to even consider, and yet, for one terrible moment, it had nearly been a reality.

"It's incredible that he saw it. But I've seen this before, my lord—on the battlefield. Some of the horses that belonged to the officers, they trusted them with their lives," Franklin said.

William nodded. "Incredibly, he spotted the traps—whether by sight, scent, or both—and stopped you. He would have done the same for your father. But in his case, it wasn't a trap. Something made him throw your father…"

His mind reeled at the possibilities.

"A gunshot…" Bella's voice was barely above a whisper, her eyes widening as a long-buried memory surfaced. "I heard a gunshot that day." She drew in a shaky breath, her face pale with the weight of realization. "I was in the parlor with Grandmère. We were reading when it happened. It was so loud that I put down my book. Grandmère commented on the hunters being too close and said she would speak to my father when he returned…" Her mouth began to tremble, and her eyes glistened with unshed tears.

William exhaled sharply, cupping her face. "A gunshot could have spooked his horse…" His mind worked quickly, connecting the pieces. "Between that and the glass shards I found in the saddle, we have to consider the possibility that your father's death wasn't an accident. But we don't know anything for certain. Not yet."

He glanced over his shoulder toward the horizon. "We're close to my manor house," he said. "Let's stop there and get some lunch."

Bella sniffled, blinking back emotion. "But what about our picnic?"

William reached for her hand. "We'll have our picnic in my study—the doors open to a scenic view of a small, enclosed rose garden," he said gently. "But I can't risk your getting hurt out here."

He gave her fingers a soft squeeze before turning to Franklin. "We need another sweep of the grounds. I thought the men had done a thorough job, but clearly, there are still traps. I won't risk the safety of my household—or Bella's. This time, I want more men. I want every inch of grass combed through—and then combed through again."

Franklin nodded sharply. "Yes, milord. I'll organize it as soon as we return."

William gave a firm nod, then turned back to Bella, his expression softening. "We'll eat first, and later, if you're up for it, we can take a ride along the beach. There's a path near the property line—it's been too long since I've kicked up sand."

Bella managed a small smile, tugging Winterborne closer. "That sounds lovely." She stroked the horse's neck. "And yes, we're still going for a ride, dear Winterborne."

Winterborne gave a soft nicker as if he understood.

As the trio walked up the drive to the manor house, a sleek black lacquered coach came into view, stationed in the drive.

"Ah… the Dormans have arrived," William said, a note of surprise in his voice. "I wasn't expecting them until later."

He could use Lucas's help with the animal traps, and he wanted to talk to him about what Bella's uncle had told him.

Turning to Bella, he added, "I think you'll like Harriett. She's a wonderful person. I met her after my cousin passed—she was the former Lady Dudley, the lady of this house." His gaze swept over the manor before returning to her. "She's here to help me refurbish it."

He caught the slight upturn of Bella's lips, and warmth spread through him. He liked seeing her smile.

And he had no doubt in his mind that his friends would adore her—as much as he did.

BELLA WAS STILL shaken from the ordeal, but the prospect of meeting William's friends brought a welcome distraction. She knew the Duke of Dorman and William had formed a close friendship through Harriett—the former Lady Dudley—who was now married to the duke.

As Franklin led the horses to the barn for water and grooming, Bella and William made their way inside to greet his guests.

The door opened, and they were met by Harlow, the ever-efficient butler.

"We've decided to have lunch here," William said. "Can you have Mrs. Bradberry set up for us in the study?" Then, lowering his voice slightly, he added, "There's also something I need your help with. Franklin is in the stable seeing to the horses, but you'll be working with him on this matter."

He quickly explained what had happened.

The poor butler went pale, utterly beside himself, immediately turning to Bella with deep concern. "My lady, I am so terribly sorry! This never should have happened. Shall I fetch the doctor?"

She offered a reassuring smile, gently waving off his worry. "Truly, there's no need. I'm fine, thanks to Winterborne."

"That fine animal has earned himself a dozen sugar cubes!" Harlow let out a breath, shaking his head in admiration. "My lord, the Duke and Duchess of Dorman arrived an hour ago. They are settling in. I will inform them that you are back and that they can join you in your study for lunch," the wiry man said before hurrying down the hall.

As Bella walked through the mansion, she took in the décor with a more discerning eye, considering the changes Lady Dorman might have in mind. At the very least, the walls would need a fresh coat of paint. The curtains and other window treatments had faded over time, their once-rich fabrics now dulled by age.

She had no intention of imposing her opinions on the duchess, but she couldn't help hoping she might offer a suggestion or two—if invited.

Entering the study, Bella blinked in surprise. It was clear the room had already undergone refurbishment, though it still retained its masculine elegance.

Rich navy velvet curtains framed the windows on either side of the grand fireplace, lending the space a sense of depth and refinement. But it was the floor-to-ceiling bookshelves, spanning three walls, that truly caught her eye.

Constructed from birchwood stained to a warm honey hue, they added a welcoming richness to the study without the heaviness of darker woods like oak or mahogany. The shelves were neatly arranged, their contents carefully curated, and rolling ladders secured to the frame ensured easy access, even to the volumes nearest the top.

The effect was both stately and inviting—a space designed for both intellectual pursuits and quiet contemplation.

A plush burgundy Aubusson carpet stretched across the floor, its intricate pattern woven with hints of blue and light gray, seamlessly complementing the room's décor.

The furnishings, crafted from a pale-toned wood—likely oak—coordinated beautifully, though they lacked the usual, yellow-tinted stain often seen in such pieces. Instead, the lighter finish lent the room an airy yet distinctly masculine feel, balancing warmth with understated elegance.

Before she could say anything, the door opened, and the duke and duchess entered.

"Lucas and Harriett, welcome," William greeted them warmly. "Let me introduce you to Lady Bella Connolly. She lives with her grandmothers and her uncle on the adjoining estate."

"It's a pleasure to meet you, Lady Connolly," the duchess said, extending a hand and covering Bella's with the other.

"You must call me Bella."

"And you must call me Harriett." The duchess was a beautiful, petite blonde with sparkling green eyes and an engaging smile.

"And you must call me Lucas," the duke said, his voice as welcoming as his wife's. Taking her hand, he covered it gently with his other, mirroring Harriett's gesture. "It's a pleasure to meet you, Lady Connolly. I can certainly see why William has been reluctant to return to London," the tall, broad-shouldered duke added, his warm brown eyes twinkling with amusement in his handsome face.

"William, did you do this on your own?" Harriett asked, gesturing around the room.

Noting the twinkle in the duchess's eyes, Bella couldn't help but like her immediately.

"I'll admit I had some help," William said with a small smile. "My housekeeper, Mrs. Aberdeen, was particularly instrumental in transforming this room."

"We had the pleasure of meeting Mrs. Aberdeen when we arrived," Harriett said. A shadow seemed to pass over her face, a brief glimpse of something distant and painful. "I only wish she had been here when I was."

Bella didn't miss the flicker of unspoken sorrow in the older woman's expression. She had heard whispers of the previous viscount—the man Harriett had once been married to—and the cruel isolation he had imposed upon his young wife.

The duke must have sensed it too. Without hesitation, he

stepped closer, wrapping a reassuring arm around his wife's waist, a silent but unmistakable gesture of comfort and protection.

"Except for the cook, Mrs. Bradberry, and the two young grooms in the stables, everyone else is new," William said. "I dismissed all the staff who made your life here miserable." His voice was gentle but firm. "It took time, but Harlow and Mrs. Aberdeen have seen to every necessary replacement. I hope you'll find your visit far more pleasant than your previous time here."

Harriett exhaled, a hint of surprise flickering across her face. "I never expected you to do that but thank you. I know now that my former husband was the one who shaped their behavior. Still…" She let out a slow breath, her shoulders easing. "It is nice to know they are no longer here."

She glanced around the room again, then smiled. "I mean it— your housekeeper has done a wonderful job. I'm beginning to wonder if you even need my help at all."

"Of course I do," William said with a grin. "Mrs. Aberdeen has an entire household to manage." His eyes gleamed with amusement. "Besides, she was quite adamant that one room was enough. I suspect I may have driven her to distraction with my tendency to keep changing my mind."

"The colors she chose are perfect—light, bright, and airy. I love it." She turned to Bella. "Would you like to work with me? We could do it together—it will be great fun. And it would be lovely to have another woman's perspective."

Bella felt heat rise to her cheeks. "I don't know… Perhaps we can take it one room at a time and see how it goes. William may not appreciate my taste."

William chuckled as he leaned toward her slightly. "I can assure you, Bella, I will appreciate anything you choose. I have seen your influence throughout your home. I have yet to see anything that isn't elegant and lovely."

She glanced at him, her heart giving a tiny, unexpected flutter. He gave her hand a gentle squeeze, his lingering smile making it clear—he meant every word.

Harriett's smile widened. "Did I hear William mention that your grandmothers are with you? They must join us for jaunts into town—for fabrics, furnishings, and everything in between. We'll have a marvelous time." She reached for Bella's hand again, giving it an encouraging squeeze. "Tell me you'll say yes."

Despite her initial hesitation, Bella found herself smiling. "Of course. I'll let my grandmothers know you've arrived—I'm certain they'll be eager to meet you."

William's expression turned grave. "I had planned to speak with both of you later, but circumstances forced us back sooner than expected. Bella nearly stepped on an animal trap—we found two. If not for her horse stopping her, she would have walked straight into one of them."

Bella felt a shiver run through her, the memory still too fresh. She had been so close to disaster.

Harriett gasped, her hand flying to her chest. "Oh my God! Those traps… They were everywhere."

Bella saw the flicker of fear return to the older woman's eyes, a reminder of what she had endured in this house.

William nodded grimly. "We found several when we first arrived, and I had my men scour the grounds. We thought we had removed them all—but we were wrong."

Harriett's expression darkened. "There were hundreds. Hidden in the weeds, among the trees—there was no escape. That was my life here." She swallowed hard, then looked at Bella. "What happened?"

If his cousin had traps set around his property, then William had been wrong about his assumption that his cousin would not be cruel to animals. He supposed his cousin's fear of losing Harriett outweighed his consideration for animals if the man would install traps everywhere—but he felt no need to mention it right now. Harriett was upset enough just revisiting the memory.

"Bella and I were riding when Winterborne—her father's horse—stopped abruptly," he explained. "At first, we weren't sure what was happening, but he kept pulling her back. That's when we saw it—the trap, half buried in the underbrush." He paused, glancing at Bella before turning to Lucas. "And that's when I realized we might be looking at her father's death all wrong."

Lucas's brows drew together. "Lord Miles Bridgewater…" He turned to Bella. "I'm very sorry for your loss, Lady Connolly. Your father was a good man. He had strong ideas and was always thinking of others. We still miss him in Parliament."

Bella blinked back the sudden sting of tears and gave him a small nod. "Thank you," she said, swiping at the ones that had slipped free.

Lucas turned back to William. "Tell me more about Winterborne and the trap."

William recounted everything—the trap, the horse's reaction, the glass shards hidden beneath the saddle, and how it had been missing from the stable after the accident. Bella added how much Winterborne had meant to her father, explaining that he was not a horse easily spooked and that her father was an experienced horseman.

"By the time the grooms reached him, they assumed he'd been thrown and struck his head on a rock," William said. "But if someone tampered with the saddle, and they thought the accident had been accepted as fact—and the saddle lost or destroyed—they wouldn't have pursued it further."

Lucas's expression hardened. "I agree. While we shouldn't jump to conclusions, this warrants a discreet investigation."

A knock at the door interrupted them. Franklin stepped inside and gave a slight bow. "My lord, the horses are settled and will be ready whenever needed."

"Good," William said. "I'll need your help organizing the footmen for another search of the estate. Harlow is aware of the situation and will assist. I want every square inch of the grounds checked for those traps. The duchess mentioned that, during her time here, hundreds were set—she was effectively held hostage in the house."

Franklin's jaw tightened. "I'll see to it immediately, my lord."

Lucas stepped forward. "I'll help with the search. I may be a guest, but just thinking about how my wife was treated here makes my blood boil."

Bella swallowed hard, trying to push past the tightness in her throat. "If one of the traps had sprung on Winterborne, it could have shattered his leg…" Her voice faltered, the weight of the near disaster pressing down on her.

"While the men handle the search, why don't we go over some ideas for the house, Bella?" Harriett suggested.

Bella nodded, grateful for the distraction. "I'd like that."

But as she followed Harriett from the room, one thought lingered in her mind—if her father's death hadn't been an accident, then someone had wanted him dead.

And that meant whoever was responsible might still be out there.

CHAPTER SEVENTEEN

"**A**LBERT GATHERED EVERYTHING we'll need for our treasure hunt, Master Michael," Stephen said, lifting a sturdy basket filled with various tools. Inside, a leather water skin, a few apples, and a wedge of cheese nestled among the supplies—just in case the boy grew hungry.

"Thank you, Lord Bridgewater," Michael said eagerly. "Can Lacey come with us?"

"Of course. Lacey will enjoy herself," Stephen assured him.

He glanced toward the tunnels, anticipation thrumming through his veins. His dream of Miles had been so vivid, so real—his brother had shown him the way, led him through the tunnels, and whispered the words that still echoed in his mind: *My death was not an accident.*

A lump formed in his throat, but he swallowed it down. Not now. Today was about the treasure.

"Where are the tunnels?" Michael asked, his wide-eyed curiosity unmistakable.

Lacey barked as if urging him on.

To Stephen, it was almost as though she were saying, *What he said.* The thought made him chuckle.

"What's so funny?" Michael asked.

Stephen crouched down, grinning. "I was just thinking of something amusing. But now it's time to get serious." He held up a finger. "First rule—we stick together. Rule number two—pretend we're pirates. And what do pirates do?"

Michael's face lit up. "Piwates have fun!" He puffed out his chest. "Lacey and me are *weady!*"

Lacey gave an excited bark in agreement.

Stephen gestured to the opening. "Then here's where we begin."

With their lanterns raised, he and Michael stepped inside, Lacey padding close at their heels. Stephen pulled the door shut behind them.

The tunnel wound and twisted beneath the earth, the damp air thick with the scent of stone and dirt. Their lanterns cast flickering light along the rough-hewn walls, illuminating shadows that danced and shifted.

"Are you all right, Michael?" Stephen asked after a few turns.

"Piwates are never afraid," Michael declared, stepping in time to a determined marching rhythm.

Stephen grinned but said nothing more. The boy's enthusiasm was infectious.

As they turned another corner, the tunnel suddenly opened up into a larger space. Shelves lined the walls, their wooden surfaces coated in dust and cobwebs.

"I wonder where all these tunnels lead," Stephen mused aloud, a flicker of regret settling over him. If only he had taken more interest in the manor and its land instead of gaming and drinking, he would have known these tunnels long ago. "We should keep going—unless you see something we ought to investigate, Mr. Pirate," he said, deferring to his younger companion.

Michael held up his lantern, considering the shelves. "No, I think we should walk," he said before setting off again, Lacey trotting faithfully behind. "How much longer, do you think?"

Stephen smirked. "I don't know, Michael. But there's treasure down here. I can feel it. Are you with me?"

Michael's eyes gleamed in the lantern light. "Yes, we are!" He marched ahead, then suddenly stopped, his lantern illuminating a darkened corner. "What does the tweasure chest look like?" he asked. "Does it have a hump on the top?"

Stephen's brows lifted. "Do you see something?" Adjusting his lantern, he directed the light toward the corner. A shape emerged—a wooden chest, its surface worn and aged, covered by so much dirt that it nearly blended into the wall.

"It's a *tweasure* chest!" Michael cried. "We found our tweasure!" He jumped up and down in excitement. "Look! It's got a lock, and it's chained to the wall!"

"That's to be expected, lad. Pirate chests are always locked," Stephen said, chuckling. He scanned the room before grabbing a hefty rock from the floor. "Let's see if we can do something about breaking it free from the chain."

With a strong, deliberate strike, he brought the rock down against the rusted chain. The metal gave way with a sharp snap.

Michael bounced on his heels. "It's *weal* exciting! Can we open it now?"

Stephen hesitated, eyeing the ornate design of the chest. "Perhaps we should wait until we get back to the manor house? That way, your grandmothers can see what you've found."

Michael considered this, his small hands gripping one of the ornate handles. "All right," he agreed.

The chest was heavier than either expected, but between the two of them, they managed to lift and carry it through the tunnel's winding passages. The musty air seemed even thicker with mystery now, and Stephen couldn't shake a nagging sense of unease.

Had they truly explored the depths of this tunnel?

According to his count of the turns, they were close to the entrance—*his* entrance. The one Miles had shown him in his dream.

Five more turns, and there it was. The lanterns illuminated the door, the large stone he had placed beside it still marking the way.

"We should hurry," he said, ushering Michael and Lacey forward. "Our lanterns won't last much longer, and I'd rather not spend the night down here."

"Arf!" Lacey barked in apparent agreement.

Stephen pushed the door open but left the marker stone where it was—in case he needed to return. "Let's get the treasure chest opened, Lord Stephen. I want to see all the gold and jewels." He turned to the dog. "Isn't that right, Lacey?"

"Arf!" Lacey seconded the sentiment.

Stephen admitted—at least to himself—that the treasure was important. He couldn't wait to see it. But would he find enough gold and rubies to pay his mother back? There was so much to fix around the manor—he needed whatever money the chest could offer. The kind of treasure he dreamed of could make a big difference in his life. And what of Elizabeth? He couldn't pursue her if his pockets were empty—especially if he was the cause. If Elizabeth suspected he was still gambling, she wouldn't want to have a relationship with him. And he dearly wanted to pursue her.

Michael stopped and looked up at Stephen. "How much farther before we can open the chest, Lord Stephen?"

"We need to keep going, Michael," Stephen said, quelling his frustration. As much as he enjoyed Michael, the boy could be wearing, he admitted to himself. But not when the little bugger was biting his lower lip with determination and trudging down the stairs, clasping the handle tightly. The two of them made it downstairs, the chest between them, just as Garrett answered the front door.

"Your Graces," Garrett said, bowing. "Lord Dudley and Lady Connolly arrived back from the stables a few minutes ago. They are in the parlor."

"Wonderful. Have you seen Lord Bridgewater?" the duke asked.

"He and Master Michael should be returning from their treasure hunt shortly," Garrett replied.

"Treasure hunt?" the duke and duchess echoed in unison.

"We have just returned," Stephen said, drawing their attention.

Harriett clapped her hands together as they appeared. "It appears you found something!"

"We need to hear more about this," Lucas added.

"And have you opened it?" Harriett asked, her voice gleeful.

"Not yet," Stephen said. "We thought we'd do that now in the parlor."

Michael grinned proudly. "I bet it's full of wubies and diamonds!" He looked around. "Where are my gwandmothers? They'll want to see the tweasure!"

"Arf!" Lacey barked in agreement.

"You're all just in time," Stephen said, leading them into the study.

⇥⟫⟪⇤

AS STEPHEN SET the chest on the desk, William stood, brows lifting. "Michael, I see you and Lord Bridgewater have found the treasure! Congratulations."

"Garrett, fetch Grandmère and Grandmama," Bella said. "Let them know Michael and Uncle Stephen found a treasure chest!"

As they waited, William, Bella, and the Dormans recounted the incident with Winterborne and the traps.

Stephen paled, shaking his head. "My God. I'm so grateful to that horse. Bella, are you hurt?"

Bella gave a small, reassuring shake of her head, but before she could respond, Stephen pulled her into a tight embrace. "You've no idea how devastated I'd be if something happened to you."

He felt the strength in Bella's embrace, the warmth of her grounding him in a way he hadn't realized he needed. The worry that had gripped him began to ease, but the weight of what could have happened still pressed against his chest.

She stepped back slightly, looking up at him. "Uncle Stephen, I'm fine, I promise. Winterborne saved me."

Stephen exhaled, his hands still resting lightly on her shoulders. "That horse is worth his weight in gold. And you—you're far too precious to lose, Bella. I've already lost my brother. I couldn't bear…" He trailed off, his voice rough with emotion, his expression shadowed by old grief.

Bella's eyes softened, and she squeezed his arm. "You haven't lost me." Her voice was quiet but steady. "I know we've been distant, but I don't blame you for anything. I want us to be close again."

Stephen studied her for a long moment before finally nodding. "I want that too." The words were simple, but there was a quiet resolve in them, a silent promise.

Bella smiled, her warmth piercing the barriers he hadn't even realized he had built.

Stephen let out a shaky breath, rubbing a hand over his face before offering a faint smirk. "Well, this has been quite the day. Between treasure hunting and near catastrophes, I think I need a drink."

Bella arched a brow, concern flickering in her eyes.

He caught the look and gave a knowing chuckle. "A proper one, mind you. Tea, perhaps. Or spiced cider."

Her expression eased, and she squeezed his arm again. "Then perhaps we should see what's in the chest first. Who knows? It might be worth toasting to."

Stephen's lips quirked into a smirk as he gestured toward the chest. "Now that, dearest niece, is a fine suggestion. I shall raise my cup of cider to whatever fortune awaits us."

With a shared glance of anticipation, they turned toward the treasure, knowing that whatever lay inside was only part of the journey ahead.

Just then, the grandmothers entered, and Michael bounced on his heels with excitement.

"It's time! Let's see my *tweasure!*"

Stephen cast one last look at Bella, giving her shoulder a reassuring squeeze before turning toward the chest, the moment between them sealed. The past could not be changed—but they had a future to mend.

Stephen lifted the hammer and brought it down in a swift, decisive motion. The lock shattered, and the lid sprang open.

An array of trinkets and gemstones gleamed inside.

Lucas stepped forward, sifting through the contents. He lifted one of the stones, turning it between his fingers before exhaling. "These are paste. There's some gold, but not much."

Stephen's stomach sank. He had hoped—truly hoped—that the treasure was real. That it might be enough to help restore the manor, pay his debts, and perhaps even change his future.

As disappointment settled over him, Lacey suddenly jumped up, paws braced against the table, eager to inspect the so-called treasure.

"Lacey, no—"

Before anyone could stop her, the chest teetered, then toppled over the edge.

Gold trinkets and paste jewels were scattered across the floor with a clatter.

"Blast it, Lacey!" Stephen groaned, kneeling to gather the fallen items.

William crouched beside him, reaching for a few of the scattered pieces. But as Stephen lifted the overturned chest, something shifted inside.

A small, hidden compartment had popped open.

Frowning, he reached inside—and pulled out a folded, time-worn document.

He turned it over in his hands, brushing off the dust before carefully unfolding it. His brows knitted together as he scanned the faded ink.

"What is it?" William asked, leaning in.

Stephen exhaled slowly, then handed it to him. "Take a look at this."

William took the parchment, his gaze sharpening as he studied the detailed markings. "This isn't just any map. It appears to be a mineral map."

Lucas stepped forward, his brow furrowing. "A mineral map? Of this property?"

The room fell silent for a beat as realization dawned.

"If this is legitimate," Stephen murmured, his grip tightening on the edges of the chest, "a corner of the family land could be hiding a fortune in copper."

CHAPTER EIGHTEEN

Dover
Two days later

"MY LADY, LORD Dudley's carriage and the Dormans' carriage have arrived. There are two carriages and they each seat six people," Garrett said, inclining his head. "I will alert the ladies and Lord Bridgewater."

"Thank you, Dudley." Bella peeked out the window of the parlor and saw William stepping down from the carriage. He looked so handsome in his buff-colored breeches and black jacket and a simple white shirt. She watched as he spoke to the duke and duchess in the second carriage. Seeing him turn back to the house, she eased the curtain back in place. She was looking forward to the fête—it was all the household had been chatting about for the past two days. Well, that and the treasure that Uncle Stephen and Michael had unearthed.

"Ah, Bella, there you are," Uncle Stephen said, stepping from his study, his face lighting up as he straightened his waistcoat. "Just a reminder that I've invited the lovely Lady Rivers to accompany us."

"Yes, I cannot wait to see her again to become further acquainted," Bella said with a smile.

She'd noticed a difference in her uncle these last few days—since he'd made his decision to stop drinking. He seemed happier, calmer, and with a spring in his step, especially where the lovely widow was concerned. Yesterday morning, he had called a family meeting and shared a codicil of her father's will with her and her grandmothers—announcing that her father had left the unentailed Bridgewater Manor to Bella, with her twenty-first birthday. What was even more noteworthy was that he declared that any mineral rights discovered on the property would also belong to Bella. Before this, Uncle Stephen had been quite evasive when it came to discussing anything about her father's will—except anything having to do with his guardianship of her.

Grandmama had suggested that he have the family solicitors examine the map to determine its authenticity, and Uncle Stephen agreed. Bella's twenty-first birthday would happen soon, but she planned to find a way to include her uncle in anything having to do with the potential copper operations. Yesterday afternoon, he had invited Lady Rivers over for tea to become better acquainted with the family—and in the case of Grandmama, to renew their acquaintance. Bella found the widow to be both spirited and kind. And it was clear—at least to the three women in the house—that Uncle Stephen was taken with Lady Rivers.

"Elizabeth lives close to where the fête is being held," Stephen said. "Perhaps I should take my smaller carriage so I can stop by her home and pick her up on the way."

"I won't hear of it, Stephen," William said as he and Michael stepped into the main hall. "Lucas and Harriett's carriage is right behind mine and has plenty of room. It's large and accommodating. It can comfortably seat six people."

"I hope everyone is ready," Grandmère said as she and Grandmama approached arm in arm.

"Wait. Lacey wants to come, too," Michael said. The black dog padded up and gave a soft woof as she planted herself beside him. "Can she, William?" the little boy pleaded.

"Since the fête takes place outdoors, it should not be a problem—that is, if Lady Bella permits it."

Michael beamed at Bella. "Can Lacey come with us, Bella?"

"I have no objection. If you keep up with her." Bella opened a closet and withdrew a leather leash. "You must keep her on her leash and close to you. And if you need assistance with Lacey, ask one of us." She smiled, handing the leash to Michael.

"I will. I promise," he said, eagerly attaching the leash to Lacey's collar. "You get to come, girl!"

Lacey gave an exuberant bark and wagged her tail.

"There's a chill in the air today, my ladies," Garrett said, handing Bella's pelisse to William. The butler smiled at Bella and her grandmothers. "If you plan to be outside all day, you will all need your pelisses."

Bella smiled at his thoughtfulness. He had always been more like a kindly older uncle or grandfather to her. Garrett had been in her father's household for what seemed like forever. His kindness had been a true comfort after her father's passing.

She couldn't help but notice that Lacey continued acting somewhat aloof around Garrett. She noticed that the dog huffed as Garrett moved forward to assist Grandmama and Grandmère with their pelisses. With so much going on, she didn't have a chance to speak to him about it. Surely they'd resolve it among themselves… at least, she hoped so.

With William's assistance, Bella slid her arms into the sleeves of her pelisse and pulled on her gloves. "I don't mind crisp weather, as long as it doesn't rain."

As soon as everyone was settled, the carriages lurched forward and headed toward town. The ladies took the first carriage, with William and Michael, and Uncle Stephen rode with the Dormans in the second carriage.

As they neared town, Bella noticed the Dormans' carriage stopping in front of a beautiful, four-storied mansion. Surrounding it were smaller, yet elegant, townhouses. Two streets separated these homes from the more popular taverns and other places frequented by the locals, yet they were all close to the beach—a reminder of the size of the town. Uncle Stephen emerged from the carriage with a spring in his step and entered the mansion. This must be the residence of Lady Elizabeth Rivers. The countess had a beautiful home.

"I suppose he plans to walk into town with the widow. It's a short distance, so it should be fine," Grandmama said. "It's nice to see my son finally more like himself."

"He's not angry or sad anymore," Michael piped up as the carriages continued on their way. "So he can be happy." The boy smiled at his grandmothers and Bella, before pasting his face against the glass, where he continued to gaze at the vast colorful tents and people.

"Michael, dear, I fear we will scatter eventually, but you need to stay with one of us," Grandmère said as they alighted from the carriage after arriving. "Grandmama and I plan to visit our friend, Madame Vorest. You are welcome to come, of course," she added.

"I would like that," he said. "Can I tell her about the tweasure?"

They all looked at William. "Perhaps it would be better to keep that to ourselves for another day or two until we find out whether the map is real," he said. "It's with the solicitors right now being evaluated. For today, we should keep it to ourselves, until we know it's legitimate."

Bella knew it was real. It had to be. But she nodded her agreement, as did her grandmothers. Gradually, Michael gave his reluctant nod as well.

"I want to try the games, and eat some of the tweats," he said.

"We'll make sure you'll get to do everything you'd like to do…within reason," Grandmama said, patting the boy's head.

"I see Madame Vorest has a tent a few yards away. What do you say we start there, Anna?" Grandmère asked.

"I'd like to see her—although it's going to be hard not to mention the treasure. Maybe we just stop by to say hello," Grandmama suggested. "Are you interested in coming with us, Bella?"

"I would like that. William, will you be with us?"

"If you don't mind, Lucas and I will be visiting a few of the tradesmen who are displaying their wares. We also want to speak to the blacksmith," William said as Lucas and Harriett approached. "Then we'll join you once more, and perhaps take some refreshment?"

"Yes, that sounds lovely," Bella said. Turning to Harriett, she asked if she would like to go with them to visit Madame Vorest.

Harriett said she remembered hearing about a Roma fortune teller when she lived at Dudley Manor, but she'd never had the opportunity to meet her and was greatly looking forward to it.

As the four women, Michael, and Lacey entered Madame Vorest's tent, they found her distraught and pacing, holding a handkerchief to her teary eyes.

"Madame Vorest, what's wrong?" Grandmère asked.

"I fear something awful has happened," the fortune teller said, wiping at her eyes. "My little granddaughter has gone missing. Yesterday, Sophia was with her older sister Diana. They were planning on walking to the home of a friend just a stone's throw away, but when her sister went back into the cottage to retrieve her gloves, she returned, and Sophia was gone. Disappeared. We searched the area all yesterday afternoon and night, and this morning. We have not been able to find her. I had to come here today, but I am afraid I am not much use."

"Have you searched the grounds of the festival?" Grandmama asked.

"Yes, as I said, we have been searching everywhere. There hasn't been a sign of her anywhere. Oh... my sweet Sophie. She's only seven," the older woman cried. "I'm certain they've taken her."

"*Who* has taken her?" the duchess asked.

"*They* have... The slavers. It's been happening for years. Dover's children have been steadily disappearing. There is a great evil in this town."

"How do you know they are being sold into slavery?" Grandmama asked.

"It is what the sailors that come here tell us—only they cannot tell us who is doing it. And we have never been able to stop it. They don't steal only Dover's children. My family… They tell me it happens in other cities and towns… even London. But so many have disappeared from Dover, and we have no idea who is behind it." She wrung her hands as she paced.

"What does your granddaughter look like?" Bella asked gently.

Madame Vorest sniffled and stared straight ahead, wiping her tears away. "My Sophie… She is my daughter's youngest child, you see. She is so pretty. She has little blonde ringlets and blue eyes, a blue like the ocean. And yesterday, she was wearing a blue dress, one that I made for her. And here I am, a gypsy. I read the tea leaves, I looked into my crystal ball, I have even tried to read my cards—but to no end. I cannot see anything. Everything is gray and murky. What good are my gifts if I cannot help my own family?"

As Bella's grandmothers and Harriett consoled the Roma gypsy, Bella whispered to Michael that perhaps he might enjoy going for a walk with Uncle Stephen and Lady Rivers—she saw them through the opening in the tent.

"I think Lacey might like to go for a walk as well," she said to Michael, who nodded solemnly.

"I'm sorry for the fortune teller," he whispered. "I hope they find Sophie."

Bella hugged him. The boy felt everything so deeply that she didn't want him to be fearful or saddened by this terrible news about missing children being sold into slavery.

Bella whispered to Harriett that she was going to escort Michael and Lacey to Uncle Stephen and Lady Rivers. "When I return," she suggested, "perhaps we can seek out William and Lucas to tell them about Sophie."

Harriett agreed. "They know a lot about these terrible smugglers. But I had no idea it had gotten this bad in Dover," she said.

"I won't be long," Bella said. "I see Uncle Stephen and Lady

Rivers at the horseshoe toss, down the way," she said, pulling back the tent flap. Taking firm hold of Michael's hand and the dog's leash, she escorted them to her uncle and told them what had happened. Stephen assured her they would watch over Michael and Lacey.

"Thank you, Uncle. I'll return to Madame Vorest's tent, where Harriett is waiting with Grandmama and Grandmère. We plan to seek out William and Lucas and tell them about the lost children," she said.

Stephen nodded. "Yes, I saw them speaking with the black-smith at the other end of the main thoroughfare."

Bella thanked her uncle and Lady Rivers again and turned to make her way back to the fortune teller's tent. Just as she was a few feet away, a hand snaked out and grabbed her wrist, yanking her to a shadowed corner.

"There you are, my darling," someone said in a low voice, a voice that made her skin crawl.

Baron Darkmoor.

Before she could run or even scream, his hand covered her mouth, and he dragged her toward a tent where several horses had been stabled.

"I heard that your family found the map—*my map*. I have been searching for it for years. That map will be mine, my dear. As you will be. When we are married, I will have both you and the treasure, something I've wanted for so very long." He yanked her hard against his chest. "And now, I would like a kiss to seal our deal, my dearest."

She tried to struggle, to get away, but he was too strong. His arms were like bands of steel around her, and he grabbed a fistful of her hair and smashed his mouth against hers in a brutal kiss. Panic engulfed her as she frantically thought about how she could get away. Anger filled her at how she had allowed herself to be taken.

She still had her feet. She remembered one of her father's grooms explaining that the top of a man's foot was a vulnerable spot. With that thought whirling in her head, she lifted her foot and, with as much force as she could, slammed her heel onto the top of his. He yelped and his grip on her loosened, and she gasped as she made her escape. But she'd only managed a few feet before he grabbed her hair and dragged her back against his chest.

"You won't get away so easily, Lady Bella. But I do like your spirit." He laughed. She almost gagged. His breath smelled like stale whisky and his lips were dry, not soft like William's. He bit down on her lip as he forced his tongue into her mouth, and she whimpered with fear as she tasted blood.

Roughly, he shoved her against a wooden post in a dark corner in the back. "You will be mine. And that is a promise," he said, as he painfully groped her breasts and forced his kiss on her again.

CHAPTER NINETEEN

"MICHAEL, WHERE WOULD you and Lacey like to go? I see a line at the treacle toffee tent. I've always enjoyed toffee. It's a little sticky, though," Stephen said, grinning.

"I've never had treacle toffee, Uncle Stephen. Before William moved me here, I had never been to any place like this. Maybe we could walk around first, so Lacey and I can look it over. Then we can decide."

"That sounds very logical, young man," Elizabeth said, gripping his hand.

"It's too bad we couldn't have had our fortunes told. I've never done that," Stephen teased. "The grandmothers say she is very good at her craft."

"I hate that Madame Vorest was so distressed, but I'm not ready to have my palm read," Elizabeth said. "I'm not sure I believe in all that hocus-pocus."

"Madame Vorest said her crystal ball wasn't working today anyway," Michael piped up.

"Really?" Stephen had never heard of a fortune teller commenting on a nonfunctional crystal ball.

"She said her visions were foggy today," Michael added. "She really misses her granddaughter, Sophie."

Of course she would be devastated. Stephen felt foolish. "I can certainly understand her sadness. I hope her granddaughter is found safe."

"Have you ever consulted a gypsy to tell your fortune?" Elizabeth asked.

Stephen gave a self-deprecating laugh. "For the last few years, I've been more used to feeling sorry for myself and giving my fortune away."

"Stephen, you were a victim of alcohol, and that made it easier for men like Baron Darkmoor to manipulate you," she whispered loudly. "I suppose I should be forthcoming. My cousin played cards with you at the Winking Mariner. He described the baron's forceful taunts pushing you to continue playing, even though you insisted that you wanted to stop. Darkmoor practically shamed you to continue. While I don't agree with his drinking and gambling, Peter has a rule, and to my knowledge, he sticks to it. He imposes a five-game limit with anyone who routinely wins in the gaming rooms. He says that Baron Darkmoor is the kind of man who pushes others beyond their limits and preys on people who cannot stop.

"That night, Peter played five hands and finally won some of his money back...and left," she continued. "He tells me that he never engages in a game with a person who's won against him five times, mostly because they probably have better skills than he does, although he added that he had heard of the baron's reputation and felt himself lucky to win one hand."

"I suppose the alcohol dulled my senses more than I realized. I didn't recognize Peter, although I knew him years ago. However, his rule is a sound one," Stephen admitted. "It's probably kept him from falling into the kind of debt that makes men desperate. It certainly happened to me." Taking a long, deep breath, he exhaled. It felt good to be able to breathe and truly smell the air around him without the haze of alcohol dulling his senses. For the first time in what seemed like forever, he felt free to re-engage in his life again. Thanks to his mother.

"I cannot understand gambling, but if Peter's rule works for him, who am I to disparage it?" She paused. "Stephen, have you heard anything from the solicitors regarding the treasure map you and Michael found? I'm just curious. That was quite a spectacular find if it turns out to be authentic. For hundreds of years, people have spoken about buried treasure here. This place was one of our summer homes and my personal favorite. We came here quite often. I was happy it was passed down to me."

"We haven't heard a thing yet. But we remain hopeful." He shrugged. "After all the financial destruction I caused my family, it would be nice to find out we have copper veins on the land— enough to repair some of the damage."

"Something smells really good here," Michael said as he and Lacey began to sniff the air around him.

"That's probably the gingerbread cakes," Stephen said. "We are close to the tent."

Elizabeth leaned down and scratched Lacey behind the ears. "I used to have a dog that looked so much like you, Lacey."

"You did?" Michael said. "She's Lady Bella's dog, but Bella's sharing Lacey with me. So, I suppose I can share her with you."

Stephen laughed. "That's so gentlemanly of you, Michael. Your timing is perfect. Lady Elizabeth and I were just talking about the treasure map we found."

"I want to talk about that… but the pirate in me smells gingerbread and beef pies. Can we have some?" Michael asked, pointing to a tent ahead of them and looking hopefully up at Stephen.

"Which? The gingerbread or the beef pies?" Stephen answered cheerfully.

Michael affected a serious look. "I would like the gingerbread first. And I think Lacey fancies the beef pie, which I would like to try, as well."

Elizabeth and Stephen both laughed, and she clasped Michael's hand in hers. "I think we can manage that," she said.

"Seems like a good idea to me. I didn't eat a big breakfast, anticipating we might find this tent," Stephen agreed. "Perhaps a glass of lemonade would be nice, as well."

Watching Elizabeth with Michael and Lacey made Stephen long for a family of his own. He was fond of Michael and would welcome a son like him, or a daughter with Elizabeth's spirit. He realized he had wasted too much of his own life being angry and jealous over his brother's life. It was time to focus on what mattered… Elizabeth and proving himself worthy of her.

She couldn't be more perfect, as far as he was concerned. She was likely no older than twenty-eight, he reasoned, recalling he was five years her senior. And she was even more beautiful and captivating than on the day he first noticed her at her coming-out ball. His feelings for her from all those years ago had never faded; he had merely buried them along with the worst parts of himself. He'd felt bitter and angry, wanting to escape into drinking, gambling, and womanizing, waiting for the pain to dull. Now he was falling in love with her. *Again.* And it was both exhilarating and terrifying at the same time. *What if she doesn't feel the same?*

The fête had taken over the common area in the town, with stalls and tents set up and down the main street and in the town's square. As they made their way to a food stall offering both sweet and savory fares, they walked by the Winking Mariner. The food stall was in the square, across the street from the pub.

"Uncle Stephen, where are all those children going?" Michael asked, pointing toward the beach. The beach extended up to a rustic wooden pier—the only barrier separating it from the town. Many businesses that locals frequented, such as the Winking Mariner, were located on the pier, with their back doors opening directly to the ocean.

A line of almost a dozen children, their heads down, shuffled toward the beach, where a boat was sitting offshore. The children were herded by three unsavory-looking men who appeared to be sailors. They looked to be heading toward the beach. Stephen's eyes narrowed as he spotted another suspicious-looking man lurking in the alley next to the tavern. *Strange…* The man looked familiar and appeared to be watching for someone. Or perhaps more than one person. Stephen's gut told him something wasn't right, but he couldn't leave Lizzy and Michael alone to investigate.

"I think that's Sophia!" Michael exclaimed, jumping up and down.

"Who?" Elizabeth asked, looking in the direction Michael was pointing to the slow-moving line of children.

"Sophia!" he insisted. "The lady in the tent was crying about her granddaughter. She was so sad. She said she was gone—those bad men had stolen her. It *must* be her. Madame Vorest said Sophia was wearing a blue dress and had yellow curls."

"Blonde hair? How old did she say her granddaughter was?" Elizabeth asked, her voice betraying her nerves. "Stephen... we must do something."

"I know, Stephen said, his mind whirling. "I recognize that shifty character lurking in the alley next to the Winking Mariner."

Michael piped up. "Lacey and I will get them."

"No, Michael, wait," Stephen said sternly. "I saw Lucas and William at that tent over there." He pointed, suddenly feeling like he needed to be two people. He couldn't leave Elizabeth, and he couldn't let the boy run around with people known to be stealing children. Looking around, it appeared the common area was mostly empty of people. "I'll watch you run to them. Do not stop anywhere else."

"We'll go straight there. I promise." With that, Michael darted off, Lacey racing alongside him. Seeing that they reached William, Stephen turned his attention back to the beach.

"We have to help these children," Elizabeth said.

"We do."

Hurrying over, Elizabeth knelt in front of Sophia. "Oh, Sophia, we're here to help you," she whispered, taking the young girl into her arms. "We're going to get you to safety, honey. Your grandmother is looking for you."

"Where do you think you're going with that girl?" a man called. "She's m'own girl. Her name is... uh... Jane."

"No, her name is Sophia, and she disappeared the other day,"

Elizabeth said in a furious voice, pulling the girl from the line.

"I'm Sophia," the little girl whispered. "My grandmother…" She glanced in the direction of the tents. "My grandmother is Madame Vorest." Holding her head up defiantly, she said, "I'm not called Jane. My name is Sophia!"

"Stop telling tales, child," the man muttered, stepping forward with his arm out as though to push Elizabeth away.

"Touch her, and you'll regret it," Stephen growled, stepping in front of Elizabeth and shoving the man away. "You work at the pub—or at least you spend most of your time there." He gave a cursory gesture, indicating the pub behind him, which sat just behind the beach's rudimentary boardwalk. "We've alerted the magistrate to these children being taken." Stephen hoped his bluff would work, or at least Lucas and William would be here in a matter of minutes.

The little boy next to Sarah spoke up. "My name's Daniel, and I'm seven years old." He had a bloodied lip and a bruise on the side of his face. "I 'aven't seen my mama and papa in two days. That's a bad man!" he said, pointing to the smuggler. "He told me he had a puppy for me if I wanted it, and then he threw me in the back of a wagon."

"Shut up," the man said, and grabbed Daniel by the shoulder.

Furious, Stephen exploded into action and drove his fist into the man's face. "Unhand that boy!"

The smuggler stumbled back, letting go of Daniel's hand. Then, with a grunt, he swung at Stephen, who ducked and shoved his head into the man's gut, knocking him down.

"Don't move with those children. Leave them right where they are," William shouted, running onto the beach where the men were marching the children to the boat as fast as they could.

Gripping the smuggler by the neck, Stephen glanced up and saw William, arriving along with Lucas and Franklin, with Michael and Lacey trailing behind.

As the five of them ran to the beach, Franklin and Lucas began fighting and rounding up the men taking the children.

Quickly, other men and women who had been walking along the beach, previously not paying attention, began to run in the direction of the children, helping them fight off three men who were shoving the children onto the waiting boat. One or two of the children seemed to recognize a relative.

The commotion on the beach only grew, and soon, the townspeople left the tents and came in swarms to help. In less than half an hour, the kidnappers were rounded up, and the children were led to Elizabeth's house, where she insisted her cook had enough biscuits and tea for the dozen or so children and the people who had helped.

"I'll be right behind you, Lizzy. Just as soon as I find out what they intend to do with these men," Stephen said. He wanted to find out more about the men he had recognized at the pub. Elizabeth was an amazing woman. He had realized it all those years ago, which had only added to his pain of loss. Now, though, she was back, and he was more determined than ever to make her his.

"The magistrate and his men have taken the men into custody," William said, walking up to him.

"Elizabeth and three of her footmen have escorted the children to Elizabeth's home," Stephen said. "We will need to find accommodations for them while we search for their families. I'm certain Lizzy will insist they all stay at her home. They appear to be between five and ten years of age, so many may not know the names of their parents."

"Thank you for stepping in, Stephen. If you hadn't, I'm not sure Lucas and I would have arrived in time. Your distraction slowed them down."

"Yes, it did," Lucas added.

"I cannot take credit. I was following Elizabeth's lead." Stephen looked at the woman ahead of him, herding almost a dozen children to her home, and immediately added *brave* to the list of reasons he loved her.

⇶⫷

HARRIETT WAS DUMBSTRUCK when Michael and Lacey returned to the tent with the little girl, Sophia, in tow. "Michael, where are Uncle Stephen and Elizabeth?"

"It's a long story, he said. "But everything is all right now."

"Everything? I'm not sure what you mean by everything." Confusion and a sudden surge of worry hit her. "Have you seen Lady Bella?" she asked, concerned for her friend.

"No, I ran and got William and Lucas and brought them to the beach, where we saw a long line of children being loaded onto a boat. I recognized Sophia from her grandmother's description."

"Brave boy," murmured Grandmère.

"I'm so proud of all of you. You could have all been seriously injured… and you, Michael, could have been taken. It makes my heart hurt to think of it all," Grandmama said, wiping away a tear.

The moment Michael and Sophia entered the tent, the young girl ran to her grandmother. The two clung to each other and burst into tears and didn't let go.

Harriett couldn't imagine where Bella had gotten to, but something felt very wrong. If she wasn't with William, where could she be? "I don't see Bella, ladies. I'll be right back," she said, leaving the group sharing hugs and tears behind her. She needed to find her friend.

As she rounded the tent that was serving as a stable, she heard a stifled scream coming from the other side. Grabbing an iron bar from a nearby tool rack, she inched her way around the tent and saw Bella being pulled against her will by Baron Darkmoor. With his hand over her mouth, he was practically lifting her off the ground and carrying her away from the fête.

Bella saw Harriett and went still, but Darkmoor didn't seem to notice her presence. Inching her way closer, she raised the iron bar and brought it down on his head, stunning him and causing him to let go of Bella.

"My God! Thank goodness you stopped him," Bella said, looking at the prone body at her feet. "He told me he was going to marry me and insisted that my house would be his, and he would finally have the treasure he'd been searching for years to find. It would all finally be his." As Bella began to realize how close she had come to being taken, she began to tremble.

"There must be a long story behind this. Perhaps we need to find William and Lucas and get this all sorted out," Harriett said, hugging and soothing her friend. "For now, I'm glad to have found you and so glad you are unharmed, Bella. I hope whoever owns the iron bar doesn't mind that I borrowed his tool. Are you going to be all right?"

"I… think so," Bella said.

For a moment, both women clung to each other. "I thought I hated my first husband, but when I saw Darkmoor pulling you away, all I wanted to do was hit him," Harriett said, smiling tremulously.

Looking down at the prone man, Bella said, "We should try to tie him up. Let's hurry," she said, grabbing some rope hanging by the door of the tent. "He's quite strong, and if he wakes up, we might not be as lucky. Had he seen you, I've no doubt he might have grabbed the weapon and tried to kidnap you, as well." A tremor visibly shook her, again.

"I wish William and Lucas were closer," Bella said. "I could use William's calm nature to settle me."

"You're probably right," Harriett said. "While William's generally a calm individual, I shudder to think what he and Lucas will do to Darkmoor when they find out what he's done. Let's hurry," she said, wrapping the rope around the baron's feet. "Everyone appears to have abandoned their tents."

"What's going on?" Bella murmured, looking around.

Shouts from the beach drew their attention. "Oh God!" Harriett said. "I was so concerned about your whereabouts that I had forgotten. Michael and Lacey came running back to the fortune teller's tent with Madame Vorest's granddaughter, Sophia. Michael said they found her along with a dozen other children being smuggled onto a boat on the beach, in front of the pub, and in broad daylight! No one seemed to notice. Had Michael not heard Madame Vorest describe her granddaughter earlier, he wouldn't have recognized the little girl and raised the alarm to Stephen and Lady Rivers. But that's all I know."

"We should get to the beach. They may need us."

BEHIND THEM, BARON Darkmoor rose and felt the blood running from his head. Seeing the weapon next to him, he realized what had happened. Quickly, he divested himself of the bindings on his arms and legs. "You may think you've escaped me, but you will find out that the baron isn't in the habit of losing anything or anyone he wants. I will have you if it's the last thing I do." Grabbing the bloodied iron, he slunk away.

CHAPTER TWENTY

Two Days Later
Cliffton Abbey

WILLIAM LAY AWAKE in his bed, staring up at the swirling center knot in his creamy damask canopy cover. He couldn't recall paying that much attention to the design of his bed before, but now that he studied it, he could appreciate the intricacies—they were much like his life now. The same intricacies that had kept him awake most of the night as he tried to weave through them.

He had anticipated that life would slow down a little with his official resignation from active duty with the Crown; instead, most especially since meeting Lady Bella Connolly, he'd felt as if he needed to grab hold, because life wasn't waiting for anyone.

Anticipating being roused early by Patrick—as his valet enjoyed doing—William had pulled his bed curtains closed the evening before, giving him a few additional moments of solitude. So much had happened in the past few days that the only way he thought to make sense of it all was to lie there and think.

The fête had been meant to be a pleasant diversion, a chance to enjoy the day with Bella and her family. Instead, it had turned into something far more startling, dangerous, and deeply worrisome.

William had spent the past two days grappling with everything that had happened—not just the discovery of the smuggling ring and the kidnapped children, but Bella's ordeal.

She had been accosted by the baron, the vile bastard who had lain in wait for the perfect moment to drag her into a darkened tent, his intentions as nefarious as they were unforgivable. Thank God Harriett had been there, helping Bella escape before something worse could happen.

But *William* hadn't been there.

That knowledge sat like a stone in his gut, heavier with each passing hour. Bella had been shaken, bruised from the struggle, but when he tried to ask her more, her eyes had darted away, unwilling to meet his.

She hadn't wanted to talk.

Harriett had promised she would speak with her, and now, two days later, William finally knew the whole story.

The baron had planned it. He had watched, waited, and struck at the opportune moment. Bella had barely managed to wrench herself free and escape his clutches.

Two kidnappings.

One targeting innocent children.

One targeting Bella.

How could two such terrifying coincidences happen in one day, at one event?

William's fingers curled into fists. He didn't believe in coincidences. And he sure as hell wasn't going to let this go.

Had it not been for Michael's keen observation, the boat would have departed with a dozen stolen children. For now, there were parents of two of the children that they were still trying to locate. It could take a while. He was thankful that Lady Elizabeth Rivers had graciously offered to shelter the little ones until their families were found.

William was also incredibly thankful and even in awe of his little brother. Michael had a keen sense of awareness. He seemed to understand not only the temperament of animals but also that of people. He had been a tremendous help with the children, calming them and making them laugh. He'd been so helpful that

Elizabeth had asked if he could stay, just in case the children had a difficult night. However, Michael wasn't ready to part with Lacey, so he declined the offer. William had laughed at that. Michael seemed to embody the best qualities of both his mother and father. William did not regret his decision to resign from the Crown to spend time with his brother one bit.

But it was Michael's conversation *after* the children had been taken to safety that still lingered in William's head this morning.

He and Lucas had been overseeing Franklin and their men tying up the smugglers.

"Very likely this is the Piper again," Lucas had remarked.

"Which makes me wonder if the Piper has been doing this right under the noses of the townspeople this whole time. What if he lives here among us? If that's the case, it would make it easier to find him..." William said.

Michael had tugged on his shirt. *"William, what is a piper?"*

Lucas and William exchanged a look.

"How long have you been standing there, Michael? I thought you were with Uncle Stephen," William said, realizing that he had been so engrossed in conversation, he hadn't noticed his brother and Lacey wander over.

Michael shrugged. *"I was, but I saw you and came to be with you. Uncle Stephen said it'd be all right. Lacey and me just got here. But you mentioned a piper. What's that?"*

William looked at Lucas, who nodded. *"We believe it's a man who is behind the stealing of the children."* Someone I mistakenly thought we had taken care of last year, he thought. *"Perhaps we've managed to capture the head of the snake this time."*

"You want the head of a snake?" the boy replied, his face contorting into a puzzled grimace.

William and Lucas exchanged amused glances.

"No, I meant that figuratively," William explained. Seeing the confusion still lingering in Michael's eyes, he continued, *"It was just a different way of saying something."*

"Well, I didn't think you wanted me to play with snakes," Michael

said. *"Do you think you can talk with normal words to me?"*

"Why did you ask about the Piper?" Lucas asked.

"Yesterday, when Uncle Stephen and Grandmama were talking, Baron Darkmoor pushed into the room and said, 'It's time to pay the piper!' He was very mean and got very mad when Grandmama gave him the money."

"You were listening at the door, again?" William asked.

Michael drew up to his full height and placed his hands on his hips. *"Well… yes. How else will I know what's going on around here? Me and Grandmère had to leave the room."*

Biting back a ready retort, William asked, *"Did Darkmoor say anything else?"*

Michael nodded. *"He said, 'This isn't over.' Grandmère and I had to move real quick because he was coming out the door where we were standing."*

It was unlikely a coincidence that the man who had attempted to kidnap Bella on the same day as the near kidnapping of a dozen children would use the same language referencing the head of the smuggling ring. William felt sure of it.

That evening, he and Lucas had penned missives to their respective contacts telling them of the events. The local magistrate had arrested five men from the fête, including two whom Stephen pointed out as regulars at the pub.

"My lord?" Patrick said, interrupting William's thoughts. "I have your bath ready. And your clothes are hanging on the stand. There's a written message from Lord Stephen Bridgewater. I'll leave it on the dresser."

Patrick sounded irritated. Probably because he hated it when William kept the curtains drawn. But had he not, he wouldn't have had a moment's peace until he finished dressing. He appreciated Patrick. He did. But the man was rooted in routine.

William sat up and pulled back the curtains. "I'm up," he said, swinging his legs over the side. "I just needed some time to ponder a few things that have happened over the past few days."

"I understand," Patrick said, sounding remorseful. "His Grace sent word that he would meet you in the breakfast room in half an hour."

Thirty minutes later, William joined his friends in the breakfast room. "Lucas, what are we missing?"

"I've been thinking of that, too," Lucas said, accepting another cup of tea.

"The five men are being held. After what they told us, I think we're closing in on the Pied Piper," William said. "Hopefully, Franklin will be back from delivering those missives tonight."

"We are so close. We just need to find a way to confirm the information those sailors gave us. We need proof," the duke said.

"Lucas, you promised we could take a walk after breakfast, and I, for one, intend to hold you to it," Harriett said, buttering her toast with deliberate precision. "I want to get to the bottom of this mystery as much as anyone, but a morning stroll with your wife is of the utmost importance."

"You are absolutely right," Lucas said, setting down his coffee. "And I certainly don't want to find myself in your bad graces." He cast her a playful look before turning to William. "According to Bella, she knocked the baron out cold."

Harriett dabbed at her lips with her napkin before giving a satisfied nod. "Yes, I did. And don't you forget it." Her eyes twinkled with amusement. "It was my good fortune to be there when Bella needed me."

William met her gaze. "You were incredibly brave, Harriett. I cannot thank you enough for what you did for Bella."

Harriett's smile softened. "You're most welcome. I would do it again in a heartbeat. Speaking of Bella, she will be here later to help me select fabrics. We would like to get your opinion, William. Oh… and we are invited to the Bridgewaters' home for dinner." She turned to Lucas. "I accepted for us."

"As you can see, my wife has many talents… one of them is taking charge," Lucas said, laughing. "I've found that it's best to do what she says."

"GOOD EVENING, GARRETT," William said.

"Right this way, Your Graces, my lord," Garrett said.

As they entered the dining room, Lacey lifted her head, made a guttural sound, and walked out of the room.

"Welcome, Lord Dudley, Your Graces. We're so glad to have you join us. We should be sitting for dinner shortly," Grandmère said. "Bella should be down soon." She paused and looked past them. "Where's Michael?"

"He could barely lift his head from all the pony riding he and Lacey did this afternoon. Mrs. Randal fed him and put him to bed—with no argument," William said, laughing. "I don't think I've seen him so tired. Not even after the treasure hunt."

"Ah, welcome, everyone," Stephen said, entering the dining room with the widow on his arm. "You all remember Lady Elizabeth Rivers."

"It's good to see you here tonight, Countess," the duchess said. "I understand many of the children you were caring for have been reunited with their parents."

"I have some exciting news on that front—news I just heard before I left," Lady Rivers said. "Two of the children were so upset, it's taken time to get them to talk. They finally started talking a few hours ago and, shortly before I left, mentioned a village about fifty miles from here."

"That's excellent news. His Grace and I would like to speak with them if you feel they are up to it," William said. "We are all hoping to return them to their families as soon as we can."

"I think they may be ready. They seem much more relaxed. I am thankful we avoided a tragedy," the countess said.

William noticed a smile pass between Lady Rivers and Stephen. He was happy for them and hoped the relationship continued to bloom. "Ah, Bella, there you are." Just seeing her smiling face lifted his mood. He had begun to worry about where she was.

"I apologize for being late. I misplaced a pearl earring but finally found it beneath my vanity. Have I missed anything?" Bella asked.

"Only that we may have a lead on where the last two children live, but we will explore that in the morning," William said, offering his arm. "You look lovely," he whispered.

"If everyone is ready, I think we can take our seats," Stephen said, Elizabeth on his arm.

As soon as they were seated, Garrett gave a quick knock and entered the room, carrying a salver. "Your Grace, a message has arrived from London addressed to both you and Lord Dudley. I thought it could be urgent, so I brought it right away."

"Thank you, Garrett," the Duke of Dorman said, accepting the missive. He read it quickly and passed it to William, who read it and nodded back at the duke.

"If that will be all?" the butler said.

Lacey glanced up from her place in the corner where she had been lying, unmoving throughout the before-dinner cocktails. Her expression was one of irritation, and she lifted her lip to show her teeth, though she made no sound.

Garrett arched a brow and shot the dog an irritated look before turning to leave.

"There! That's exactly what I've observed repeatedly," William said, tucking the message into the pocket of his waistcoat and leaning back in his seat. "Before we turn our attention away from our topic of discussion, this… behavior between the butler and the dog…" he began. "It's worsening. If he yelled at her, as Bella says, for sneaking treats to Winterborne—which I find adorable—how can the rift be mended? Every interaction I've noticed seems to be getting worse. A week ago, they seemed the best of friends. Now… this." He gestured casually toward the dog in the corner, whose only response was to grunt and close her eyes. "She seems content with it."

"Garrett was quite harsh in his admonishment. I believe he

should apologize, and I've told him so," replied Grandmère, eyes twinkling with undisguised mirth. She picked up her glass and took a sip of wine.

"I wasn't present for it, but I gathered from Mrs. Bisque that Garrett had set aside the apples for himself, and Lacey helped herself to them without notice or permission," Grandmama said, biting her lip to suppress a laugh.

The duchess barely suppressed a titter until Bella joined in, and then the two ladies erupted into fits of giggles.

William bit his cheek in an effort not to join them. "I suggest we hand this issue over to Michael, as he appears to understand both animal sensibilities and human perspectives."

"I second that suggestion...not because I think you a bumbler, but because you have described your younger brother's talents perfectly," the duke said, laughter shining in his eyes, as he raised his glass of wine.

"Hear, hear," the group chimed in between laughter and giggles.

⭇

AFTER DINNER, STEPHEN stood and gained everyone's attention. "Thank you all for agreeing to join us tonight. I would like to thank the viscount and his dear friends, the Duke and Duchess of Dorman, who have helped us immensely."

"It has been our pleasure to join you. And our friendship is readily given," Lucas said.

"Thank you," Stephen said to the room.

William studied him carefully, noting how he gripped the back of his chair as if grounding himself. Gone was the reckless man who had squandered opportunities and left his family to mend his failures. Tonight, Stephen appeared different—burdened by his past but finally ready to take responsibility.

"I invited you all here tonight to offer my sincerest apologies and to clear up any misunderstandings." He hesitated, his gaze sweeping the room before he exhaled. "The blame for our family's entanglement with the dreadful Baron Darkmoor lies with me."

At the mention of the baron, William's jaw tightened. His gaze flicked to Bella. She sat in composed silence, her hands gently clasped in her lap, but he caught the slight curl of her fingers—an unconscious sign of tension.

Stephen continued, his voice steady but edged with regret. "I wallowed in self-pity, resenting my brother's successes instead of standing beside him. And in my weakness, I made choices that put us all in danger."

William already knew all of this. Stephen had confessed his mistakes to him days ago when it was just the two of them. But this—standing before the gathered room, exposing his faults for all to see—was something else entirely. A man who had spent years avoiding responsibility was now owning his failures.

But William wasn't thinking about Stephen.

He was thinking about Bella.

She had already forgiven Stephen. She had already moved past the betrayal. But that didn't erase what had happened. She had been through an ordeal—one that still lingered in the unspoken spaces between them.

At the village fête, Baron Darkmoor had nearly taken her. If not for Harriett's quick thinking, Bella would have been lost to them. And the baron—*damn him*—had escaped.

Guilt gnawed at William. He hadn't been there. Instead, he had been on the windswept shore, stopping the smugglers and rescuing a dozen helpless children. He had done what needed to be done, but that didn't change the truth—he hadn't been there for her.

Across the room, Bella lifted her gaze, meeting his.

His breath caught.

There was no anger in her expression, no blame. Just quiet understanding. And something deeper—something that made his chest tighten.

Love.

It was there. He could feel it, as surely as he felt the weight of his own feelings for her.

Whatever words Stephen spoke next faded into a dull hum in William's ears. Nothing mattered in that moment except the woman across the room. The woman who had nearly been taken from him.

The woman he would never—*could* never—let go.

Stephen continued, recounting everything that had transpired with Baron Darkmoor and the role his mother had played in helping him. His voice remained steady, though the weight of his words settled heavily over the room.

Around the table, several people drew in a deep breath, the tension palpable. The enormity of what had happened—of what had nearly happened—hung between them like a storm that had barely passed.

Stephen turned to his mother. "I cannot thank you enough, Mother. I love you," he said, his voice thick with emotion as he embraced her.

Grandmama clung to her son, tightening her arms around him as she dabbed at the tears gathering in her eyes. "Oh, my dear boy," she whispered, her voice trembling.

For all that had been lost, for all the pain that had been endured, in that moment, something had been mended.

William smiled. "It seems this is the perfect moment to reveal my own secret, Bella."

He watched as curiosity flickered in her eyes.

"When you visited Cliffton Abbey, you noticed a rather pungent perfume on me—one, I assure you, I did not enjoy." His lips quirked, but his tone remained serious. "What you didn't know was that the night before, I had gone undercover. I was following your uncle, trying to piece together what was happening in town."

Bella's expression shifted, but she remained silent, listening.

"Though I resigned from actively working with the Crown, I still have my connections. That night, I played cards with your uncle, hoping to gain insight—not just into his dealings, but into the trouble surrounding your family." His gaze went around the room. "Especially since I had Michael to think about, too. And he had already become so attached to all of you."

Stephen's face reddened. "I had gotten rather foxed, I'll admit. So much so that your secret identity will remain safe with me."

William snorted. "Bella, I was so tired, I fell asleep. And I smelled atrocious. You were right to get angry."

Bella lowered her gaze, a flush rising to her cheeks. "I remember that morning. I was awful to you," she admitted softly. "Forgive me. I had no idea."

William regarded the beautiful young woman who held his heart. "Bella, there is nothing to forgive. You only reacted to what you knew at the time. I should have explained sooner." He reached for her hand. "All that matters now is that you know the truth."

"Does anyone have anything else to share?" Grandmère asked. "My goodness! This was so much easier than gaining my information through keyholes."

Everyone laughed.

"Cheers, dear family and friends!" Stephen said, lifting his glass of water. "There's nothing better than family and good friends."

"Cheers!" Lady Elizabeth Rivers said.

"Cheers!" the grandmothers added.

AFTER DINNER, LUCAS approached William. "So, the office confirmed our suspicions," he said in a low voice.

"They did," William murmured. "We need to find him."

CHAPTER TWENTY-ONE

Bridgewater Manor
The next morning

"UNCLE STEPHEN! GOOD morning! Would you like a cup of tea?" Bella asked, surprised to see her uncle up so early. He usually slept in until late morning.

Stephen slid into the seat across from her, offering a warm smile. "I'd love some tea, Bella. It's nice to have a quiet moment—just the two of us."

She set a steaming cup in front of him and he added a spoonful of sugar. His gaze shifted to the tray of fresh pastries, and his smile widened. "I see Mrs. Bisque has made her famous apple cinnamon scones—my favorite." Taking one, he took a bite and let out a satisfied sigh. "Mrs. Bisque never disappoints."

Bella grinned. "I agree. I asked her to make an extra batch for Michael, William, and the duke and duchess." She reached for a scone herself. "I thought I'd take a basket over when I meet with Harriett. We're going over fabric swatches for the parlor at Cliffton Abbey."

Stephen nodded. "Ah, sounds like a productive morning. Are you walking over right after breakfast?"

"I thought I'd go out to the stable first and spend time with Winterborne. Ever since Michael identified what had been wrong with him, I've felt a sense of relief but also guilt for not realizing just how deeply the loss of my father had affected him. That he'd basically lost his best friend. Animals bond with their humans and aren't able to flip their feelings on and off any faster than we can. While I was mourning my father's death, with my family's support, poor Winterborne was left to grieve essentially on his own, with no one to help him through it."

"I'm sorry to hear that Winterborne was suffering so deeply," Stephen said. "I hadn't realized it either. We think of animals as property, but they are so much more." He looked over at Lacey, who was seated at Bella's feet. "Take Lacey and Garrett, for example. We all hope they can somehow overcome this rift between them. Still… it's over apples," he said, his lips twitching.

Bella tried not to giggle as she thought about the butler and her dog squabbling over treats for her horse. "Yes, sometimes conflicts that can be easily handled are taken too far. I agree."

He cleared his throat. "That reminds me. There's something I wanted to share with you—about the conflict Miles and I once had."

She hesitated. "You don't have to, Uncle. I… I know you and Papa argued before his death."

Stephen exhaled. "We did, and I shall carry that regret for the rest of my life. But… perhaps your father and I have come to a sort of understanding."

Bella frowned slightly. "What do you mean?"

He met her gaze. "Miles visited me in a dream. And it was not an easy dream to have."

She set down her teacup, all thoughts of breakfast forgotten. "What did Papa say?"

"In the dream, Miles took me on a journey—down into the tunnels—to tell me about the treasure. And before you think it too far-fetched, what he revealed to me did come to pass, almost exactly as he described."

Bella sat perfectly still, her pulse quickening. A dream about her father? And the tunnels?

"Miles wanted me to understand several things. At first, he was frustrated with me—and rightfully so. I had failed you in ways no decent parent would forgive. I let the baron gain the upper hand, and that devil demanded I betroth you to him. Your father was furious. He didn't raise his voice, but there was no mistaking his ire."

Bella's fingers tightened around the edge of the table. She had always known her uncle carried regret, but hearing it now, spoken so plainly, made her throat tighten.

Stephen reached for her hand, his grip firm but warm. "But believe me, Bella, he was no angrier than I was at myself. I resisted the baron's demands, but I was too lost to my vices—gambling and drinking. I had no way out. No way to protect you, no way to save myself."

Bella swallowed hard, her father's presence in the room suddenly palpable. Whether a dream or something more, the idea of his still watching over her sent a shiver down her spine.

"Miles told me that there was treasure, and I needed to find it—but he didn't say what kind, just that it would take care of us. He guided me through the tunnels and told me I had to complete the journey myself. And the next day, when Michael and I explored the tunnels, it was as I remembered it from my dream! Your father made certain we'd find the treasure, I'm sure of it. But the dream... It was the most amazing experience I've ever had in my life, and I was *sober!*"

They both chuckled lightly at that.

"I've heard back from the solicitors—the map is authentic. We can begin exploring the copper veins... if that's what you want. The property is rightfully yours."

Bella shook her head. "No, Uncle, this treasure belongs to both of us. We can put that in writing."

Stephen studied her for a long moment before nodding. "I don't want you to feel obligated to share it with me. But we can discuss the details later."

She took a slow sip of tea before setting her cup down thoughtfully. "Papa once told me he believed in your talent as a painter."

A flicker of something—surprise, perhaps even gratitude—passed across Stephen's face. "That means more to me than I can say... to know that he had faith in me." He let out a self-deprecating chuckle. "Though I'm not sure I ever deserved it."

"Why didn't you pursue it?" she asked gently.

He sighed, rubbing his jaw as if trying to put years of regret into words. "That's a good question. One I've been asking myself a great deal lately. Painting was the only thing that ever truly brought me happiness—well, that and Lizzy. When I stopped, I became... unmoored."

His gaze turned distant as if he were looking into the past. "My father was a difficult man. He thought painting was a foolish pursuit, even for a second son. He wanted me to be more like Miles—practical, sharp-minded, capable of shrewd investments. He never hesitated to tell me so, and in time, I let his voice shape me. I tried to be more like your father. But the truth is, I never wanted to be the earl. I never coveted his title. Miles was born to it, and he carried it well."

Stephen swallowed hard, his voice rough with emotion. "I loved your father, Bella. I would give anything to have him here again. But abandoning my passion—trying to force myself into a role that never fit—made me bitter. Resentful. Angry at my father, at Miles... and, in time, at myself."

He hesitated, then continued. "And then I lost Lizzy. She married a man with a title, a man who could give her everything I couldn't. I turned to drink. I let jealousy fester—jealousy that Miles had married for love, that he had you, a daughter he adored. He surpassed even our father's success, and yet he remained good-humored, devoted to his family, and endlessly kind. My brother was everything I was not. And I resented him for it."

Bella's chest ached as she listened, the weight of his regret settling between them.

"Then Miles died," Stephen went on, quieter now. "And suddenly, I was forced into the very role I had spent my life avoiding. Becoming the earl only made me more of a stranger to myself. I blamed everyone else for what my life had become. And I fell deeper into vice, into anger, into the clutches of men like the baron."

He let out a breath, shaking his head. "I see it all now—how lost I was. Thanks to your grandmother's kindness and forgiveness, thanks to Miles's visit in my dream, and to Lizzy's unwavering spirit, I am beginning to find my way back. But Bella, I must ask for your forgiveness as well. For the way I treated you. For not being there for you in your grief. For allowing the baron into our lives."

"Thank you, Uncle Stephen. You have my forgiveness—you always have. And my support. My love." Bella's voice softened. "I only ever wanted you to see what we all see—that you deserve happiness, too."

Stephen's expression was unreadable for a moment before he reached out, patting her hand. "Thank you, Bella. That means more than you know. You are every bit Miles's daughter. I know how proud he was of you."

She sniffled, dabbing at her eyes. "I'm sorry. I don't seem to be able to stop weeping."

Her uncle chuckled and handed her his handkerchief. "Well, your father was known to get dust in his eyes from time to time as well."

A soft woof sounded under the table, and Bella looked down to see Lacey placing a gentle paw on her foot, her soulful eyes filled with quiet concern.

Bella giggled, reaching down to scratch her dog's head. "You lovely, sweet girl. Thank you, Lacey."

"There's one more thing, Bella," Stephen said, his voice turning grave. "Before your father faded from my dream, he told me his death was not an accident."

Bella's breath caught, her eyes widening in shock. "I—" She swallowed hard, her mind racing. "That is a shock to hear, but… I've begun to think the same, Uncle. Especially after what happened the other day—Winterborne saved me from the traps. He put himself in danger rather than let me fall into one."

She shook her head, the weight of realization settling over her. "We misjudged him—all of us. I know, in my heart, that he would have done everything possible to prevent Papa from falling, to keep him safe. Even if we never learn the full truth, I believe that much."

Stephen nodded, his own eyes gleaming with unshed tears. "Perhaps one day, we will. I want to look into it—and with William's help, maybe we can find out who was behind this vile act."

Bella took a steadying breath and nodded. "I'll do whatever I can to help. But Uncle... Papa wouldn't want us to lose ourselves in grief or vengeance. He would want us to live, to find happiness." She gave him a pointed look, a soft smile playing on her lips. "You must pursue your dreams—whether that's painting or, perhaps, a certain lovely widow."

A flicker of something lighter passed across Stephen's face, but Bella continued with conviction. "I believe Papa visited you in that dream to remind you of that—to encourage you to live the life you were meant to live."

He nodded. "What if I join you in a little while? I have a couple of things to tend to in my study. When I finish, perhaps we can go for a ride."

Bella smiled. "I'd love that, Uncle Stephen."

The Bridgewater stables

"WINTERBORNE, COME HERE, fella," Bella called, waving a carrot enticingly. The handsome gelding pricked his ears and trotted to the stall door, his dark eyes bright with recognition.

She had begun to think of him as hers—because surely that was what Papa would have wanted.

As she stroked Winterborne's velvety muzzle, her thoughts drifted to her own horse, still at the Bridgewater family estate in Hertfordshire.

Duchess.

The beautiful white mare her father had given her on her sixteenth birthday. She had hoped Uncle Stephen would bring her here, but he hadn't. Now, she understood why. Even so, she would have to speak to him about it again. She missed Duchess—missed the steady companionship of her gentle-hearted mare. And she knew, deep down, that Winterborne missed her too.

Duchess had always had a calming presence. Bella was certain she could help Winterborne as well.

She absently stroked the horse's forelock, already imagining the day the two horses would ride together again. Perhaps Grandmama would join her—she still rode on occasion. She had always been an excellent horsewoman. They could exercise both horses, a comforting thought that brought a small smile to Bella's lips.

"Arf!" Lacey barked, nudging an apple toward Winterborne with her nose.

Bella laughed. "Are you stealing Garrett's apples again, you little thief?" she teased, scratching behind the dog's ears. "You're such a sweet girl. You were the only one who kept Winterborne company all those months. I think that deserves a proper reward." She tapped her chin thoughtfully. "Perhaps an extra bone from the kitchen? I'll have to ask Mrs. Bisque to set one aside for you."

Leaning down, she kissed Lacey's soft black nose. The dog grinned up at her, eyes full of knowing mischief, as if to say, *I knew you'd come around. We were both just waiting for you to feel better.*

The sun had just risen, the air was crisp, and a layer of light frost covered the bushes and grassy area around the stable. They were alone. It was Bella's favorite time with her horse—even when they were back in Hertfordshire.

As a child, she would watch from her window as her father put his horse through its paces, the two moving together in perfect harmony. Those quiet moments belonged to them alone. Then, when no one was looking, she would slip outside to visit the other horses, whispering secrets into their ears and sneaking them carrots and apples.

The memory tightened her throat with emotion. Her conversation with Uncle Stephen had stirred old grief, bringing tears to her eyes—but it had also warmed her heart. For the first time in years, she felt truly close to him.

"I do feel better, Lacey and Winterborne. It just took me a while," she murmured, handing each a treat from her pocket. Winterborne finished his apple and grabbed the carrot from her hand. Lacey enjoyed the cheese that Mrs. Bisque had wrapped in a napkin for her.

As Winterborne leaned in for another apple, he suddenly jerked back, tossing his head violently. A shrill scream tore from his throat as he reared, slamming his hooves against the wooden stall in a frenzy of agitation.

Bella barely had time to turn before arms wrapped around her from behind. A damp rag, reeking of laudanum, was pressed hard against her mouth and nose.

Panic exploded through her. She struggled, twisting against the iron grip, but it was too late. The sickly-sweet scent filled her lungs, making her head swim. Behind her, wood splintered as Winterborne thrashed, his cries of rage piercing the air.

A low, cruel whisper brushed against her ear. "I killed your father to get this house—to own the mine rights."

Bella let out a muffled cry, jerking her head, trying to break free, but his grip was relentless.

"Even with glass beneath his saddle, the stupid beast refused to throw him," Darkmoor sneered. "So I forced his hand. One shot from my pistol, and he went down. He was groggy but alive—until I finished the job."

His laughter sent ice through her veins. "One good blow with a rock, and it looked like an accident. And now, Bella, it's all mine—you, the property, and the copper."

The rag pressed harder, stealing her breath and forcing the drug deeper into her lungs. Spots danced in her vision. Her ears rang with the sound of Winterborne's screams and Lacey's frantic barking—until she heard a sudden, furious growl.

"Damn dog," the Baron spat.

Before she could react, she heard the sickening *thud* of his boot making contact. Lacey let out a sharp, pained yelp as she hit the wall and whimpered, the sound cutting through Bella like a knife.

No!

She tried to fight, tried to force herself to stay conscious. But the laudanum dragged her under, her limbs going slack as darkness swallowed her whole.

CHAPTER TWENTY-TWO

Bridgewater Manor

WILLIAM AND MICHAEL had just crested the hill dividing the two estates when shrill cries and panicked screams split the air. A horse.

Then he saw it—a thick plume of black smoke billowing from the Bridgewater stables.

"My God! The stable is on fire." William's pulse thundered. He turned to Michael. "Ride to the main house—now! Alert everyone. We need all hands to put out the fire and get the animals to safety. Make sure no one stays inside in case the flames spread."

Michael gripped his reins tightly. "But I can help—"

"You *are* helping." William's voice was firm. "We need the household warned immediately, and I can't have you near the fire. Now go!"

Michael hesitated for only a second before nodding, then spurred his pony toward the house at a gallop.

William didn't waste another moment. He swung off his horse and ran toward the stables, the acrid scent of smoke burning his lungs.

Through the thick haze, movement near the paddock caught his eye.

Winterborne.

The stallion had broken free, his muscles taut with fury. His ears were pinned back, nostrils flared, teeth bared as he lunged at Baron Darkmoor. The massive horse snapped at the man's arm, forcing him to drop Bella to the ground.

But the baron wasn't safe yet.

Winterborne reared, hooves pounding the dirt with furious intensity. Darkmoor staggered back, eyes wide with shock, struggling to stay upright. He was strong, but against the unrelenting wrath of an enraged stallion, he was powerless.

William surged forward, his only thought—*Bella*.

As he drew closer, he saw Lacey dragging herself toward her mistress, barking hoarsely, as if trying to wake her. When Bella didn't stir, the dog let out a distressed whimper and curled over her, a small, fierce protector shielding her from further harm.

"She's mine, you stupid beast," the baron spat, breathless and enraged.

William's blood turned to ice as Darkmoor yanked a pistol from his coat and aimed it at Winterborne's head.

"I should have killed you a year ago," Darkmoor growled, his face contorted with fury, his cheeks flushed a deep crimson.

William didn't think—he moved.

In an instant, he grabbed the baron by the collar and yanked him back, throwing his full weight into a punch that smashed against Darkmoor's face. The baron staggered, dazed—but before he could recover, William tackled him to the ground, fists flying.

Blow after blow, William drove his knuckles into the baron's face. He barely registered the crunch of breaking bone beneath his fists—he just kept hitting.

"I'll get Bella out of here!" Stephen's voice cut through the chaos.

With one final, bone-shattering punch, William knocked the baron unconscious. He turned just in time to see Stephen pass Bella into the waiting arms of a footman.

"My God, man! We saw the smoke and came to help," Lucas called, reaching William's side. "I brought Franklin and your footmen. Harriett is organizing the fire brigade, and we've sent

Franklin for the doctor."

"*No!*" Stephen's scream split the air.

William spun just in time to see Darkmoor grabbing his pistol again. The barrel lifted—aimed directly at William.

Before William could answer, Stephen hurled himself at the baron just before a shot rang out.

Darkmoor collapsed under the weight of the attack.

Stephen went down hard, blood seeping through his shirt and covering his side.

William and Lucas rushed to his side. "Stephen—damn it, stay with me," William said urgently, searching for the bullet wound. "I found it. It's in his shoulder."

Despite blood pooling on his sleeve, Stephen rolled over and let out a weak breath. "I'm still with us," he muttered.

William pressed a firm hand to the wound. "We'll get you out of here."

As they carried Stephen to safety, William's mind churned with thoughts of those he loved—Michael, Bella, and their grandmothers. He prayed they were all safe. But most of all, he prayed Bella would recover.

They laid Stephen on the grass as Harriett rushed up with medical supplies.

"Bella… is she… all right?" William asked Harriett, his voice sounding hoarse to his own ears.

"She's breathing, and that's a very good sign," Harriett said, bending to clean Stephen's wound with the help of a maid.

William forced himself to stand, his focus shifting. "We need to get back and make sure that fire is completely put out, or it could spread."

Lucas hesitated, glancing at his wife, who gave him a reassuring nod. Then he turned to William. "Let's go."

How he wanted to see Bella. Needed to. But there was too much to do. And too many people rushing about. He barely caught a glimpse of her—lying on a blanket, surrounded by her grandmothers, Michael, and Mrs. Bisque.

Bella. She was all he could think about while pummeling the baron. Just seeing her in the bastard's arms had filled him with an unrelenting fury.

He hadn't even told her how much she meant to him. How much he loved her. Yes. He did love her. He realized that now. But they had to make sure the fire was put out. It was why he'd been a good agent for the Crown. His ability to stay focused, no matter the circumstances.

As he and Lucas ran toward the burning stable, Garrett's commanding voice rang out over the chaos.

"Take the prisoner to the gardener's shed," the butler called, motioning toward Darkmoor's unconscious form. "Lock him in, put shackles on his hands and feet, and gag him. One of you stand guard while the other brings me the key."

"Yes, sir." The footmen moved quickly, binding the baron and hauling him away.

William couldn't help but be impressed. Garrett had issued his orders with the precision of a seasoned general.

And then William saw something else that quite astonished him: Garrett knelt and gently scooped Lacey up into his arms. He murmured something low, and as he pressed a gentle kiss to her head, she gave a small wag of her tail. The battered but resilient dog leaned into the butler and licked his chin.

William shook his head, allowing himself the barest flicker of amusement.

It seemed Lacey and Garrett had finally settled their differences.

But there was still work to do. Before he could take Bella into his arms and tell her just how much he loved her.

BELLA OPENED HER eyes and, for a moment, stared into the sooty faces of William, Grandmère, and Garrett. She glanced by her side and saw Lacey, her back leg bandaged, but resting comforta-bly. Her dog was safe and sound. *Thank God.*

"How do you feel, Bella?" William asked gently, a tender smile on his face.

She gazed into his incredible blue eyes that looked even bluer in his soot-covered face and felt her heart do a dozen flip-flops.

"Thirsty," she said, her voice sounding ragged.

Grandmère handed her a glass of water. "Take small sips."

Bella nodded and drank as much as she could.

She tried to focus, as the words were all jumbled up, waiting to be said at once. Taking a deep breath, she started. "He killed Papa," she said, wiping the sudden tears that rolled down her face. "I was afraid I might never wake up and be able to tell you what he said he'd done. He pressed a handkerchief to my mouth… I think it was laudanum. But before I fainted, he told me that even with the glass he had placed beneath the saddle, Winterborne wouldn't throw Papa, and that was when he fired the gun…"

"I remember a gunshot that day," Grandmère said. "My God!"

"I do, too," Bella said weakly. "If only we'd had some inkling of what he was planning. Winterborne recognized him… and that's why he reacted so violently at the stables today. All this time…"

"You need to get your strength back," William said, lifting her hand to his lips.

If Bella hadn't already felt faint, she would have likely swooned right there as William placed a soft kiss on her fingers. "Where are Uncle Stephen and Grandmama?" she asked.

"Stephen is in his room with Grandmama and the doctor," Grandmère said. "A bullet passed through his shoulder—and the doctor was able to make sure there were no fragments. He should make a complete recovery."

"I'm so relieved," Bella said.

"Uncle Stephen jumped on the baron when he was trying to

shoot William," Michael said. "He's a hero."

Bella's eyes widened at that declaration. "Is that true?"

William rolled his eyes at his brother. "Let's keep Bella as calm as we can for now, all right, Michael?"

Michael nodded, but his eyes danced with mischief.

"Are you hurt?" Bella whispered.

"I'm fine," William said in a reassuring tone.

"Lady Bella, I am so happy to see you awake," Garrett said as he walked up to the group gathered around the settee.

"Thank you," Bella said.

"Garrett, you're a hero too!" Michael exclaimed. "William said you saved Lacey." He nodded at the small black dog snoring at the end of the settee. "And you're no longer sore at each other," he added, a wide grin on his face.

Garrett cleared his throat. "Yes, well, Lacey is a valiant dog, and she was very brave protecting her mistress. And for that, she has my undying gratitude." He reached down and patted the dog on the head.

"Come along, Michael—I think Mrs. Bisque has some warm milk and cake for us," Grandmère said, with a wink at Bella and William. "Garrett, won't you join us? I want to hear all about how you took charge in that barn."

"Yes, madam," he said with a smile as he followed Grandmère and Michael out of the parlor.

"Do you hurt anywhere, Bella?" William said, moving closer to her on the settee. "I felt so helpless when I saw you lying there."

"I'm sure I don't hurt as bad as the baron. I understand you broke his nose and part of his cheek, and Winterborne broke his legs," she said.

"Indeed. I think your horse would have killed him if I hadn't arrived when I did. Come to think of it, I was very near to doing that myself." He shook his head. "Can I get you anything?" he said softly as he caressed her cheek.

Despite how good his touch felt, Bella couldn't stop from

grimacing. "Oh, that hurts," she said, holding her stomach. "Remind me never to almost get kidnapped again by an evil baron with a handkerchief soaked in laudanum."

William poured her a cup of tea from a teapot on a side table. "Here, take a sip of this. Mrs. Bisque brought it in just before you woke up."

Bella took a few sips and began to feel better.

"I've known a few soldiers who stay away from opiates for the same reason," William said. "I'll keep that in mind... and make sure the doctor never gives it to you."

Bella's eyes widened. "You will?" She giggled. "How do you plan to do that?"

"By marrying you, of course." Grinning, he went down on one knee. "Lady Bella Connolly, will you do me the honor of becoming my wife?"

Bella covered her mouth, afraid to say anything. "I'd have to speak to Uncle Stephen. I'm not of age yet..."

"Already done. And your uncle has given us his blessing," William said.

"Even so, I should check on him..."

"You're going to make me wait for an answer?" William asked, with an arch of his brows.

She bit her lower lip and gazed up at him with an impish grin, which elicited a groan from him that made her smile even wider. "I would love to become your wife, if you will kiss me... and make it one of the good ones."

"There's nothing I'd rather do." William bent and captured her lips in a heady kiss. "I love you, Lady Bella Connolly."

"And I love you too, Lord William Dudley," she said, sighing.

He pressed his lips against hers once more, and as their breaths mingled, their tongues met in a teasing, sweet dance, while his fingertips ran alongside her jawline, and he looked into her eyes. The rest of the world faded away, leaving only the heat between them and the quiet hum of pleasure as their lips clung together, exploring, teasing, and tasting. It was a kiss that sealed their love and reaffirmed the promise of a future together.

EPILOGUE

A year later
Bridgewater Family Cemetery

WIPING TEARS FROM her eyes, Bella brushed off the leaves from the bed of her father's and mother's graves. She felt a quiet sense of peace knowing her parents were together. She took immense comfort in that—even though she felt the loss of their passing every day.

Today marked the second anniversary of her father's death, and the questions surrounding his death had finally been put to rest. His death had been intentional, part of Baron Darkmoor's evil plot to seize her father's land and control her. Thankfully, that was thwarted partly because of the protective influence of her father's spirit.

It had been almost three years since her sweet mother had succumbed to the wasting disease. Her father had wanted her final days spent in Dover with a peaceful and relaxing view of the sea. Sadly, they lost her only a month after they arrived. As much as Bella had hated leaving their country estate in Hertfordshire, where there were so many memories of Mama, she finally understood her father's decision to make this her final resting place. Upon standing here and looking out at the ocean, Mama declared this her favorite place on earth.

Glancing over her shoulder, she saw William, holding the leads of Winterborne and Duchess, and felt the familiar, powerful feeling she always experienced here, a feeling that he was the person her parents had always wanted for her.

She rose and went to him. "Perhaps Winterborne will find a similar sense of peacefulness near Papa," she suggested, taking the reins of her horse.

"And how about Duchess?" he asked, smiling, his eyes crinkling with laughter.

"I think Papa would find great delight in what has unfolded with my horses," she replied, laughing too. When Duchess arrived at Bridgewater Manor, she developed an unmistakable fondness for William, which Bella found utterly amusing. Particularly because Duchess made her preference known whenever Bella would try to saddle her. She would look at William with the most soulful eyes and whinny, finally calming down when he approached.

One day, Michael had blurted over dinner, "Duchess looks at William the way you look at Bella," in front of the grandmothers.

To which Grandmère said with a cheeky smile, "And what way is that, Michael?"

Michael fluttered his eyelashes and heaved a deep sigh. "*Ahhh*... Like that," he said, giving his best imitation of a sigh and fluttering eyelashes from Bella.

The table erupted in laughter, as they all realized that the horse *had* taken a fancy to William. Since William didn't have a preferred horse, he was open to the idea of taking a favored horse. And it seemed Duchess was determined it would be her.

As they neared the gravestones now, a gentle breeze stirred the air, rustling the golden leaves of the nearby oak. The wind lifted those that had settled atop her parents' gravestones, sending them into a slow, swirling dance. Around them, dandelions and the pale violet blooms of winter heliotrope swayed in quiet harmony, their soft whispers merging with the hush of the moment.

Bella and William exchanged a glance, a silent understanding passing between them, their eyes reflecting the same quiet awe.

Then, as if attuned to something beyond their senses, Winterborne stepped forward. The stallion let out a low, resonant neigh, dipping his head toward her father's grave—as though he were listening to a voice only he could hear.

"How remarkable. It's almost as if the leaves are whispering to him in the wind," Bella murmured.

"Perhaps they are," William said, pulling her close.

"If I close my eyes, I can smell my mother's fragrance—jasmine," she said, looking up at him and smiling.

"I smell it too, and I've never smelled it so strongly. Is that why you wear the jasmine fragrance, darling?" he asked. He leaned in slightly. "It was one of the first things I noticed about you—beyond your generous spirit, your beauty, and a few other things I fully intend to worship tonight," he added in a low whisper, his eyes gleaming with promise.

Heat flooded her cheeks. Even after almost a year as husband and wife, William still had the power to make her blush—both with his words and the way he looked at her.

"Mother gifted me a bottle of her jasmine fragrance on my sixteenth birthday," she admitted softly. "I've loved it ever since. And now, it makes me feel closer to her."

The clip-clop of a horse's hooves sounded behind them, and they turned as Uncle Stephen dismounted. "I thought I'd find you here," he said, approaching the gravesite. Looking down, he shook his head. "I feel such a wash of bitterness, anger, and guilt over Miles's death."

"Papa's death was not your fault, Uncle Stephen," Bella said, taking his hand. "The baron was determined to get his hands on the property no matter what. Besides, Papa would ask you to put those feelings behind you and live your life in happiness and peace. He always knew what was in your heart."

"But the drinking and the debt…"

She shook her head as tears came to her eyes. "It was a sickness—as much as the illness that claimed Mama. You had nothing to do with his dying. That was the baron's plan. He already wanted this property—and my father was in his way."

"Bella is right," William said. "For your peace of mind, you must put it behind you."

Stephen gave a slow nod as he digested the words. "I would like to set my bitterness aside," he finally admitted. "Your hearts are so generous—both of you, Bella and William…"

"Uncle Stephen, you are Papa's heir and the rightful earl. You are the head of the Bridgewater family now. And nothing the baron attempted to do damaged or erased that."

Stephen heaved a deep sigh. "Speaking of the baron, that's why I came to find you both. I stopped at the house first, before I came to the graveyard. Harlow said this missive had just been delivered from the duke. I offered to bring it to you," he said, handing the note to William.

William opened the missive and looked from his wife to his brother-in-law. "The Pied Piper was hanged yesterday for the murder of your father. As much as I hate to condone the death of any man, Baron Darkmoor was one of the most evil men I have crossed paths with. Justice has finally been served."

Bella shivered as the wind picked up and the leaves floated once more above the gravestones. For a long moment, the three of them gazed at the sight in front of them, as Winterborne continued to neigh softly over the graves.

"He misses Papa so much," Bella said, her voice almost a whisper. "In many ways, Winterborne was my father's final gift to me. But there's a gift I'd like to share while we are all here…with Papa and Mama."

William gave her a curious look. "Is it…?"

She nodded, smiling brightly. "I am with child. I've kept it quiet until I knew for sure. Our child will be born in the late spring."

William gave a cheer and, lifting her in his arms, whirled her around in a circle—then stopped himself. "I must take care. You have to be careful from here on out." He set her down gently and, keeping his arm around her shoulders, gave her a tender kiss.

Bella giggled. "Winterborne agrees with you." The horse looked up at them and nickered. "I think he already sensed I was with child. He was most adamant about going slowly this morning. Whenever I tried a light canter, he gave me a most frustrated look and refused to go faster."

Both men laughed.

"Perhaps we should consult Michael on that. The boy has an uncanny ability to understand animals…and people," Stephen said.

"What do you think about naming the child after Papa if it's a boy or Mama if it's a girl?" Bella asked in a hopeful voice as she gazed up at her husband with love.

"Miles would have loved that," Stephen said. "But he would never have expected it. All he wanted was what I want… for you to be happy. You've both been extremely generous to me, entrusting me with overseeing the mine and its operations and giving me a share. I never expected that. And inviting me to live at Bridgewater Manor. Now I spend all my time at the mine and painting."

"We are happy, Uncle. Now it's time for you to follow your dreams and do what makes *you* happy."

Stephen gave a sheepish smile. "I shall try." Then, with a sudden spark of excitement, he added, "And to that end, I must be off. Lizzy is expecting me to help choose the flowers and decorations for our wedding." He let out a small chuckle. "To be honest, I'm enjoying every second of it—because it means I get to spend more time with her."

Bella couldn't help but smile, seeing the happiness she had long hoped for finally displayed in his eyes.

After Stephen had left, William turned to her. "I cannot tell you how happy I am about the baby," he said, reaching out to caress the curve of her cheek. "You are the person I never knew I needed—until you quite literally fell into my arms that day. I have loved you ever since. And now, to think we will have a child… I must confess, I'm a wee bit anxious. I pray I will be a good father."

Bella's heart swelled at the vulnerability in his voice. "You will be wonderful," she assured him. "I see how you are with Michael. You are a natural."

William exhaled, some of the tension in his shoulders easing. "I promise, I'll do my best to make sure both you and our child are happy."

"Speaking of Michael, Mrs. Randal tells me that he hasn't had any more nightmares—not since we gave him one of Lacey's puppies," Bella said.

"Ahh! Another brilliant idea of my lovely wife," William said, kissing her on the nose. "With a black star on her forehead, I don't think he could have come up with a better name for his white puppy than Star."

They both laughed.

William tucked her closer to him.

Bella tilted her head and looked up at him, her face suddenly serious. "You won't mind if it's a little girl? I dreamed of a little girl just last night—a golden-haired, green-eyed child laughing as she played with Lacey on the beach."

William chuckled. "No. I'd love a green-eyed daughter who looks just like her mama, with her mother's heart and spirit."

Bella's throat tightened with emotion. "And I've known since that very first moment we met that you were the one for me, William Dudley," she confessed, her voice trembling. "You are my anchor, the very center of my life. I love you deeply."

She slipped her hands up around his neck, tilting her face up to his. "But right now, all I crave is to silence the world around us and lose myself in your kiss."

"Gladly!" William pulled her close with a sudden urgency that mirrored her own.

As William lowered his lips to hers, a rush of warmth enveloped Bella, stealing her breath. His kiss was both familiar and electrifying, soft yet insistent, his lips moving with a gentle persistence that sent shivers down her spine. Their tongues met in a sensual dance—exploring, tasting, and deepening the connection that had always existed between them.

Her senses were filled with the feeling evoked by the touch of his hands tracing slow, reverent paths up and down her back and the intoxicating scent of him—sandalwood and citrus, warmth, and home.

Behind them, Winterborne and Duchess neighed happily, their presence a quiet blessing in the golden afternoon. Bella pressed herself closer, reveling in the solid strength of her husband, in the love that bound them.

William groaned softly—a sound that sent a thrill through her, awakening every part of her heart and soul. As their kiss deepened, the world around them blurred into nothingness. There was no time, no space—only the heat of their love, burning bright, unshakable, endless.

~The End~

(or *maybe not.*)

About the Author

Anna St. Claire is a big believer that *nothing* is impossible if you believe in yourself. She sprinkles her stories with laughter, romance, mystery and lots of possibilities, adhering to the belief that goodness and love will win the day.

Anna is both an avid reader author of American and British historical romance. She and her husband live in Charlotte, North Carolina with their two dogs and often, their two beautiful granddaughters, who live nearby. *Daughter, sister, wife, mother, and Mimi*—all life roles that Anna St. Claire relishes and feels blessed to still enjoy. And she loves her pets – dogs and cats alike, and often inserts them into her books as secondary characters. And she loves chocolate and popcorn, a definite nod to her need for sweet followed by salty…*but not together*—a tasty weakness!

Anna relocated from New York to the Carolinas as a child. Her mother, a retired English and History teacher, always encouraged Anna's interest in writing, after discovering short stories she would write in her spare time.

As a child, she loved mysteries and checked out every *Encyclopedia Brown* story that came into the school library. Before too long, her fascination with history and reading led her to her first historical romance—Margaret Mitchell's *Gone With The Wind*, now a treasured, but weathered book from being read multiple times. The day she discovered Kathleen Woodiwiss,' books, *Shanna* and *Ashes In The Wind*, Anna became hooked. She read every historical romance that came her way and dreams of writing her own historical romances took seed.

Today, her focus is primarily the Regency and Civil War eras, although Anna enjoys almost any period in American and British history. She would love to connect with any of her readers on her website – www.annastclaire.com, through email – annastclaire author@gmail.com, Instagram – annastclaire_author, BookBub – www.bookbub.com/profile/anna-st-claire, Twitter – @1AnnaSt Claire, Facebook – facebook.com/authorannastclaire or on Amazon – amazon.com/Anna-St-Claire/e/B078WMRHHF.